Meadow side

Meadowside

ISBN-13: 978-1497459571
ISBN-10: 1497459575

http://marcusblakeston.wordpress.com
marcus.blakeston@gmail.com

Prologue

Wilson Duppoint pulled the key from the ignition and stepped out of his silver BMW into the torrential rain. Silently cursing his luck at having to park so far away from the shopping centre entrance, he hurried across the car park. Stinging rain thudded against his back, plastering his thin white shirt against his skin like a cold, clammy sponge. It poured down his bald head and dripped from his nose. He licked his lips. The rainwater had an odd chemical taste he couldn't quite place, a bit like licking a battery but without the mild electric shock.

The constant hammering of cold water droplets against his head brought on a dull, throbbing pain between his temples. He could feel it getting worse with each step he took. The chemist would need to be his first port of call, he decided. Some Nurofen would soon sort him out, then he could hit the rest of the shops pain-free and concentrate on finding the perfect anniversary gift for his wife.

A blinding flash of white light filled his vision. A pain more intense than anything he had ever felt before lanced through his skull. He had a sudden urge to look up at the sky, and did so. He didn't blink. Not even when huge drops of water pounded into his eyes. He stood immobile, letting the rain wash over his face. The pain melted away.

Then he heard the sound. Awful, harsh. Like the squeal of a thousand dying rats fed through an echo chamber on a continuous loop. He knew he had to find whatever was causing that sound and silence it. He growled low in his throat as he looked around for its source. He sniffed the air. There were others nearby, he could sense them. They shuffled together, slow and methodical, making for a glass-fronted building close by.

Wilson Duppoint staggered forward to join them, his legs stiff and unresponsive as if he had forgotten how to walk. As he approached the building he could see things moving around inside. The things that were making that awful noise. A swarm of them, mocking him with their incessant screeches. He bared his teeth and hissed at them to stop. Others nearby joined in his call. Together they would silence them. Tear them apart. Destroy them.

There was another urge too. It was just the faint glimmer of an idea at first, but soon became an all-encompassing primal yearning. He wanted to know what they tasted like

1

Kylie knew she had to have those yellow Nike trainers as soon as she saw them on the shelf in Sportswear Direct. They were the best trainers she had ever seen, Trisha and her gang of skanks on the council estate would go mental when they saw her wearing them. They'd be jealous as fuck, and so would everyone else.

Kylie plucked the trainers from the shelf and turned them around in her hands, admiring them from all angles. She ran her finger over the raised logo and smiled to herself. There was no doubt about it, she would look the fucking bomb wearing those. She sat down on a nearby padded bench and kicked off her skanky no-brand trainers, wishing it could be for the last time ever. Wishing she could toss them into a burning skip, never to see them again.

The amount of ribbing Kylie got from the other kids on the council estate over those horrible trainers was unbelievable. Like it was Kylie's fault her mother would rather spend the child allowance on booze and ciggies. She'd begged for months and months for a proper pair of trainers, then got yelled at for not being grateful when her mother came home with those awful things instead.

Pumps, she called them. "There's nothing wrong with pumps from the market, they're just as good as the ones you want. You should be fucking grateful, I didn't have to buy them, you know, and I never got nothing like this when I was your age."

Yeah well, she wasn't the one who had to wear them out in public. But Kylie was going to put that right soon enough. She glanced at Tom and Mike, who were running around the shop dribbling a basketball to each other, attracting the overweight security guard's attention. That just left the cameras to worry about.

The security guard told Tom and Mike to pack it in and

get out of his shop. Tom laughed and told the man to piss off. The security guard made a grab for the basketball, but Tom and Mike ran rings around him, passing the ball back and forth between them and laughing at the fat man's clumsy ineptitude.

Kylie smiled. It was definitely worth blowing out her dad for his weekly Saturday afternoon access time to go to Meadowside with Tom and the others. She was getting a bit too old for visits to the local zoo anyway. Who wants to go and look at miserable-looking smelly animals with some old geezer when you can have fun like this with your mates instead? Dad would just have to get used to the idea Kylie wasn't a little kid any more.

Kylie dropped the new trainers and slid her feet into them. They were a perfect fit, just like she knew they would be. She stared down at them, rotating her ankles to get a better look. They were the fucking bomb all right. She bent down and tied the laces, then straightened up to see what the trainers were like for walking. It was like walking on air.

Kylie made her way through Sportswear Direct, past displays of tennis racquets, golf clubs and hockey sticks, into the clothing area. Britney was there with her Spongebob Squarepants backpack, looking a lot fatter than she had when they first entered the shop together. Britney winked when she saw Kylie walking toward her. Kylie nodded back and made for a full-length mirror. She turned around and craned her neck over her shoulder, trying to see what the new trainers looked like from the rear.

"Nice shoes," Britney said. Kylie turned and smiled. She looked at Britney's over-stuffed pink tracksuit and wondered what goodies it contained. "They look like they'd be good for running, yeah?"

Kylie shrugged and looked down at the yellow trainers, suddenly afraid of the consequences if she got caught stealing them. She remembered the last time she had been caught shoplifting. That look of fear on her mother's face at the sight of a police officer on the doorstep. The mixture of relief, fury and disappointment when she realised they weren't there for her. And then the beating Kylie got for bringing police to the house. She didn't want to go through all that again. But at the same time she knew she would never hear the last of it from Britney if she bottled out now.

"Yeah, I guess," she said with a frown.

Britney winked. "Well come on then, let's test them out, yeah?"

Britney turned and strode away. She waved to Tom and Mike, who were still dodging around the security guard with the basketball. Mike nodded, then they both lured the security guard further into the shop while Britney made for the exit.

Kylie looked up at a security camera and sighed. Her heart hammered in her chest at the thought of being caught again, but she was determined not to let her fear show. She closed her eyes and tried to steady her breathing until she could get her racing heart under control. She jumped at a loud clatter and looked around. Tom or Mike had thrown the basketball at a display of golf clubs and knocked them off the shelf. The security guard shouted at them, red-faced, while he picked the golf clubs up. Tom and Mike ran for the exit together.

An alarm sounded when Britney passed through the shop's security barrier. Its shrill, piercing siren made Kylie jump again. She ran for the exit herself, her arms pumping by her sides.

"Oi, you lot," the security guard shouted. Kylie could hear the man's laboured breath behind her as he gave chase.

Kylie ran like she'd never run before. Even on that cross-country run a few months ago when her sadistic PE teacher had been right behind her shouting abuse like some world war two army drill instructor she hadn't run this fast. Her lungs felt like they were on fire, and a pain in her side felt like someone had stabbed her with a red-hot poker, but she didn't dare stop running. She darted around bemused shoppers, following Tom and the others as they veered left onto another concourse, then barged past people on the escalator down to ground level. She ran past the bronze war memorial statue and the wishing fountain where people with more money than sense tossed their unwanted pound coins, then into the big department store near the train station exit.

Britney, Tom and Mike were laughing when she caught them up. They had slowed to a casual saunter past rows of clothing designed for old women. Frumpy purple dresses nobody in their right mind would want to be seen dead in. Silly hats like the ones the posh people wore when they went for a day at the horse racing. Awful green cardigans for grannies too senile to know any better.

Britney pulled a green and yellow hat with a floral design from a shelf and placed it on her head at an angle. "Look at me," she said, spinning before Tom and Mike, "I'm a fucking lady."

Tom laughed and shook his head. "Girl, you're no fucking lady."

"Piss off," Britney said, pouting. "I am too a fucking lady." She took off the hat and tossed it away.

Kylie panted, desperate to get her breath back. She bent over and clutched her aching sides.

"Check it out, I'm a fucking lady too," Tom said in a high-pitched voice.

Kylie looked up and couldn't help smiling. Tom had a big floppy pink hat on his head, with a matching pink fluffy scarf draped over his shoulders. He pinched the chest of his Adidas T-shirt in both hands and stretched it out, forming pointy breasts.

"We should ... we should get ... going for the train," Kylie said. "Before ... we get caught by ... that security guard."

"Nah," Britney said. "He'll have given up long ago, the fat ones always do. Besides, if he chased us for too long everyone else in the shop would run off with loads of stuff so it wouldn't be worth it."

"Even so ..."

"Fucking intense, weren't it, Kylie?" Tom said. "And them new trainers of yours look fucking smart."

Kylie looked down at her new trainers and smiled. They'd got a bit scuffed from the run and had lost a bit of their new-shop shine, but they still looked good. She lifted them in turn and polished them on the back of her tracksuit bottoms. Then she remembered her old trainers were still in the shop. She looked up at Tom, her eyes wide.

"We need to take them back, say it was a mistake or something."

"What? Don't be daft, what would be the point of that?"

"But I left my old ones behind, they'll know they're mine."

Tom snorted. "What, like in fucking Cinderella or something? What are they going to do, take them round the council estate and see who they fit?"

"They might have DNA in them, or fingerprints? Footprints, even."

"So what? They still wouldn't have anything to match it with, would they?" Tom took off the pink hat and placed it on Kylie's head. It was way too big for her, and flopped down over her eyes. "There you go Kylie," he said, "you're a proper fucking lady now, too. So stop worrying."

Kylie lifted the brim of the hat over her eyes and smiled at Tom. That was the sweetest thing anyone had ever said to her, and she wanted to reach out and grab him, plant a massive kiss on those lips of his.

But Tom turned away before she could do it. "Come on then Lady Kylie, let's get fucked off out of here," he said, walking toward the exit. Mike and Britney followed him, hand in hand. Kylie took off the hat and put it back on the shelf when a woman at a nearby till glared at her. She smiled at the woman and shrugged, then hurried to catch Tom up.

It was raining outside, a heavy downpour that bounced off the pavement. Black clouds filled the sky.

"I ain't going out in that, it's fucking pissing it down," Britney said, pulling off her Spongebob Squarepants backpack. "We'll get fucking soaked if we go out there."

"Yeah, fuck that," Mike said, shaking his head. "We'll wait until it stops."

Hidden behind Tom and Mike, Britney pulled out the clothes she had stuffed inside her pink tracksuit and transferred them to her backpack. She had gone for top designer brands, and Kylie sighed when she saw their labels. Britney was sure to be the envy of the entire council estate when she wore those, and Kylie's new trainers would barely get a second glance next to them.

"Look at that daft bastard," Mike said, pointing.

A bedraggled-looking man stood outside, looking up at the sky. Rain bounced off his face, but he didn't seem to care.

Tom laughed. "Oi mate, you're getting wet," he shouted through the door. If the man heard Tom from outside, he didn't acknowledge it. Tom shook his head, grinning, then turned to Kylie. "Well I don't know about you, but I'm with Mike and Britney. No way am I going out in that. We'll wait and see if it eases off first."

"So what are we going to do then?" Kylie asked.

Tom smiled and took her hand. "Let's go and see what's on at the cinema. I've got a mate who works there, he'll get us in for free."

2

Amy Saunders couldn't believe her luck. For over five years her and Ryan had been trying for a baby, with nothing but monthly heartbreak to show for it. Something wrong with her fallopian tubes, the doctor explained, but Amy was too busy sobbing into her hands to listen to the details. It was Ryan, stoic as ever, who asked what their options were.

The doctor suggested IVF, and Amy looked up with renewed hope, wiping the tears from her eyes. But that hope was soon dashed when the doctor said she was too old to qualify for NHS treatment. He was, however, more than happy for her to proceed as a private patient, and rubbed his hands with glee when Ryan said money wasn't an issue.

The treatment failed, and Amy wept into Ryan's arms when they were told none of the embryos produced were viable enough to be implanted. Most had simply stopped growing in the lab's incubator, something Amy was told was common. Those that survived all had chromosomal abnormalities, and had been destroyed.

Undeterred, Ryan took on a second job, working a combined total of fifteen hours per day, seven days per week. With Amy's own job, working in the offices of a meat processing plant, they hardly saw each other. They scrimped and saved, and sold anything they could do without, so they could pay for another round of IVF six months later.

The second treatment also failed, so they took out a secured loan to pay for a third, putting their home up as security. This time, miraculously, it was a success, and Ryan had fussed over Amy non-stop ever since. If Ryan had his way Amy would have been confined to bed for the entire pregnancy, with doctors and nurses on hand twenty-four hours a day.

But Amy knew better. She had read all the information in the New Mother's Welcome Pack she picked up at the chemist, and knew she could carry on working for at least another seven months, maybe even longer. Which was just as well, considering the amount of debt they were in, and all the new things they would need to buy for the forthcoming baby.

And now here Amy was, in Mothercare, looking at baby-grows, buying last minute items in preparation for the big day. Just two more weeks and the round lump Ryan had christened Bumpy would be cradled in her arms wearing one of these outfits. The nursery was all prepared, decked out with the best equipment they could afford. They hadn't wanted to know Bumpy's sex, they wanted it to be a surprise, so the nursery had been decorated with neutral colours, the cot mobile chosen because of its genderless dangling farm animals.

A baby-grow with green scales caught Amy's eye and she picked it up, smiling at how cute the gurgling baby on the packaging looked wearing the outfit. The baby looked like a tiny smiling dinosaur, with built-in scratch-mitts designed to look like claws, and a hooded crown-cap with large buggy eyes printed on the sides. There was even a small tail growing out of the back of it, with a bright yellow triangle of soft material at its tip. Ryan would love this one, Amy decided. He was like a big kid himself as far as dinosaurs were concerned.

"You'll love it too, won't you Bumpy?" Amy said, rubbing her hand over her distended stomach. As if in reply, the baby wriggled inside her. Amy smiled. "That's good enough for me."

She hummed a tune to herself as she took the baby-grow to the pay desk. Then a movement outside the shop caught her eye. She turned to look. A small group of people ran by. Amy shrugged and turned back to the counter. She placed the dinosaur baby-grow down in front of the young woman who stood there.

"Oh, that's so cute," the shop assistant said, scanning a barcode on the packaging. "How long have you got now?"

"A couple of weeks," Amy said, smiling. "I've already started having Braxton Hicks, and I can't wait."

The woman smiled back as she placed the baby-grow in a carrier bag. Amy took out her purse and paid for it, then took the bag and turned to leave.

"Bye then," the shop assistant said, "have a nice day."

"You too," Amy said, still smiling to herself.

A woman ran by outside the shop, casting furtive glances over her shoulder as she ran. She looked terrified of something. Amy stopped and watched the woman through Mothercare's shop-front window until she was out of sight. More people ran past, shouting and screaming. Amy glanced quizzically at the shop assistant, who just shrugged in reply.

Amy turned back to the window. A middle-aged bald man in a blood-specked white shirt stared in at her. His hands were bloody, his face too. His eyes were wild and staring, as if he were in shock.

"Are you okay?" Amy asked, raising her voice.

The man lunged at the shop window with a snarl. Amy startled, then stepped back in horror as he hit the glass face first with a dull thud. His head bounced off the glass and he staggered back a few steps before launching himself forward again. His nose shattered against the glass. He reared back for another charge and left behind a dripping red smear.

Amy screamed. She backed away, unable to take her eyes off the man as he repeatedly launched himself at the window, impervious to the pain he must be causing himself. She dropped the shopping bag and raised a hand to her mouth.

Blood poured down the man's face as he continued battering his head against the window. Then he stopped

13

and pounded on it with his bloody fists instead. The window shuddered in its frame with each blow. He bared his teeth and snarled like a dog. He stared in at Amy with malevolent, bloodshot eyes, then resumed banging his head against the glass.

Amy didn't know how much more of this punishment the window would take. She didn't understand why the man hadn't already rendered himself senseless from the repeated blows to his head. And why didn't he just walk through the door instead?

An ice-cold shock of fear ran down Amy's spine. She spun to face the shop assistant in panic.

"The door!" Amy shouted, her eyes wide. "You need to lock the door!"

The assistant stared past her, open-mouthed, at the man pounding on the window. Amy walked up to her and shook her by the shoulders.

"You need to lock the door before he gets in!"

The assistant shuddered, then blinked several times. She shook her head slowly. "What?" she asked, her voice barely audible over the noise the man outside was making.

"The door," Amy yelled. "Where are the keys?"

"The ... keys ...?"

"Yes, the keys. Where are they?"

"I ... they're in my pocket."

Amy released the woman's shoulders and reached into her uniform's left hip pocket while she stood immobile, staring past her, her face deathly white. Amy pulled out a bunch of keys and looked at them. They were labelled main door, alarm, store room and staff toilets. She shuffled the main door key to the fore, and turned back to the shop front.

The window shattered inwards. The man stumbled and fell into the shop. He writhed around on the carpeted floor, glass shards tearing through his clothes and slicing into his flesh. Amy and the shop assistant both screamed simultaneously. The man snarled through blood-stained teeth and pushed himself up onto his hands and knees. Glass sliced through his wrists and sent red arterial blood spurting. He crawled toward Amy and the girl, leaving a thick trail of blood behind him.

Amy backed away, brandishing the keys at the man as if they somehow held the power to stop his advance. She sensed, rather than saw, a movement behind her. The shop assistant ran past, heading for the entrance door. She wrenched it open and ran out—

—straight into the grasping hands of another man lurking there.

She cried out and beat at the man's head with her fists, raked her fingernails down his face. The man snarled and lashed out at her, knocking her sideways into the window frame. A jagged shard of glass still clinging to the frame pierced her neck and her screams turned into a choking gurgle as she coughed blood. The man grabbed her shoulders and pulled her down. The glass shard tore up through her neck, then came loose from the window frame and fell with her.

The man dropped down to his knees and pulled out the large sliver of glass, slicing through his own fingers as he did so. He threw the glass to one side and lowered his mouth to the gaping wound in the girl's neck. He slurped and smacked, drinking the life-force pumping from her veins with relish.

Amy watched it all from inside the shop. She trembled in fear, frozen in place, unable to tear her eyes away from the horror outside. Her legs turned to jelly. She reached out for the counter to steady herself. Something warm and wet ran down her legs and soaked into the carpet. Amy didn't have time to worry what that meant. A snarl came from close behind her, to her right. The man in the suit crawled toward her, a look of determination on his battered

15

and bloody face.

"Help me," Amy yelled when she saw someone running by outside the shop. But the running figure didn't even look in her direction.

The man in the doorway looked up and hissed. The shop assistant's blood dripped from his chin as he locked eyes with Amy. He stumbled to his feet and stepped through the broken window, his arms swinging by his sides.

Amy backed further into the shop, unable to look away. Something dug into her back. She cried out and spun around, fearing the worst, expecting to come face to face with another psycho lurking within the shop. Expecting her life to end at any moment in a savage attack she would be powerless to defend herself from. But it was just a clothes rail, filled with coat-hangers displaying brightly-coloured maternity dresses.

Amy reached out and grabbed the clothes rail to steady herself. She felt it move on tiny wheels as she leaned against it. The man lumbered toward her. As he got closer he reached out with both hands, his fingers grasping. Amy backed away, edging herself around the clothes rail. When she reached its far side she pushed it as hard as she could in the man's direction. The man hissed in anger when the clothes rail collided with him. His hands flailed at the maternity dresses, pulling them from their hangers. One wrapped around his face and he roared as he thrashed around, trying to free himself from it.

Amy ran to the back of the shop, where she saw a solid wooden door bearing the sign Staff Only. She pressed down on the door's handle frantically. Then cried out in frustration and banged her fist on the door when it refused to open. Angry snarls came from behind, the sound of coat-hangers clashing together, garments ripping.

Amy remembered the keys she had taken from the shop assistant, and uncurled her fingers from them. Her hands shook as she located the store room key and inserted it in the lock. The key turned impossibly slowly, as if time were coming to a standstill. Amy wrenched down the handle and stumbled through into the store room, almost losing her footing. She tried to pull the key from the lock but it was stuck.

The man was close. Very close. Amy was sure she could feel his breath on the back of her neck as he hissed and snarled at her. She screamed and tugged at the key. She glanced over her shoulder. The man was even closer than she thought, only a few feet away. Wide-eyed and hysterical, Amy wrenched the key from the lock and slammed the door behind her just as the man lunged at the doorway.

But the door wouldn't close. The man's fingers curled around its edge, trapped in the doorway, flexing and unflexing. Amy pulled the door open a couple of inches and slammed it back. Bones crunched and the fingers stopped moving, but the door still wouldn't close fully. The man hissed again. Amy heard scratching sounds, as if he were trying to claw his way through the wood. She leaned her shoulder against the door and pushed with all her might, barging it into place. A severed finger slithered down the door and dropped by her feet. The others hung down from flaps of skin holding them in place. The man pounded on the door, his guttural snarl turning into a wail of anger.

Amy put the key in the lock and twisted it. She leaned back against the door and slumped down to her knees, sobbing with her head in her hands while the man's pounding vibrated through her back.

Then her stomach tightened, like the worst menstrual cramps she had ever felt. She cried out and clutched herself. Tears ran down her face as she panted through the pain, knowing there was a lot worse to come.

3

Kylie had seen 18 rated movies on TV, but none of them had been as intense as the one she watched in Meadowside's cinema. She didn't understand why Tom was more interested in playing on his phone than watching the movie. He'd been tapping away on it all the way through, giving a running commentary on what he found people saying about the movie on Twitter.

Bare Knuckle Bitch, the movie was called. The poster outside the cinema described it as a romantic comedy with lashings of ultra-violence, the perfect date movie for feral underclass. Kylie found that an accurate description. Abby, the movie's main character, was certainly one tough bitch who took no shit from anyone, but she had her gentle side too. Abby's best mate, Shaz, reminded Kylie a bit of Britney the way she acted around boys sometimes, and Abby's skinhead boyfriend had a little bit of Tom's loveable goofiness about him.

Britney seemed to be enjoying the movie too, and cheered Abby on as she stuck the boot into some toffee-nosed students who had been giving her some lip earlier on. Mike laughed and sneered, saying three blokes, even wimpy ones like those, would be more than a match for such a skinny looking bird as Abby. But Kylie knew better. It wasn't strength that mattered in a street fight, it was what you did with your fists and your boots. Kylie's arms and legs twitched as she imagined herself in the movie, punching and kicking someone unconscious just like the girl on the cinema screen.

Then Tom nudged Kylie in the ribs and broke her concentration. "Check it out," he said.

"What?" Kylie whispered. She didn't want to look away from the screen. The posh students were covered in blood, lying groaning in the street while Abby rifled through their pockets and stole their wallets.

"There's some sort of riot going down in Shefferham," Tom said, holding up his phone. "Check it out."

Kylie glanced at Tom's phone and shrugged. "Yeah, so?" She turned her attention back to the movie.

"Let's get down there," Tom said.

"What for?"

"For the looting, what do you think what for? Shit's just there for the taking when there's a riot going on, I've seen it on the telly."

"Yeah?" Britney said, leaning forward to look past Kylie at Tom. "I could do with a new phone, my old one sucks."

"I don't know if we should," Kylie said, shaking her head. "There'll be coppers everywhere, and people fighting, we wouldn't want to get caught up in all that."

"Nah," Tom said, "the coppers aren't doing fuck all, Twitter says so. People are just smashing stuff up and getting what they can. Come on, let's get down there before all the good stuff's gone."

Britney picked up her Spongebob Squarepants backpack and shuffled to the exit, closely followed by Mike.

Kylie frowned. "But I want to watch the rest of the movie," she said to Tom. "Don't you want to see how it finishes?"

"Nah, it's boring. I'll download it for you later, you can watch it on my laptop."

Kylie sighed. She didn't really want to go, but it seemed like everyone else had already made their mind up. And she *had* always wanted a laptop of her own, so maybe she could get one from the riot?

"Well okay, if you're sure it'll be safe?"

Tom smiled. "Yeah, we'll be fine. We'll just go down there, get some stuff, then get fucked off out of there before the coppers change their mind and start laying into everyone." He stood up and looked down at Kylie. "Come on then, let's get going."

Kylie took a final look at the cinema screen and made her way to the exit door, where Mike and Britney were waiting. They pushed through into the lobby and headed for the main exit. Tom stepped through first, and collided with a man running past outside. He was knocked off his feet and sprawled to the ground. The man continued running without looking back.

"Are you okay?" Kylie asked. She reached down to help Tom up.

"Yeah. Some people have just got no fucking manners." Tom glared after the running man and shook his head. "Fucking wanker."

They set off in the same direction as the running man had gone, past the food hall where delicatessens and salad bars competed with burger joints and tea rooms, and back into the main shopping centre. More people ran by. Someone screamed in the distance. Kylie cast a worried glance at Tom, but he just shrugged and led the way to Meadowside's train station exit.

A young woman, her hair and clothes drenched from the rain, staggered toward them swinging her arms. A small baby strapped to her chest in a harness made an odd rasping sound and raised its tiny arms. Its eyes were wide and staring, its face screwed up in hate. Its mouth opened and closed, making the gurgling, hissing sound undulate. As the woman stumbled closer she bared her teeth and hissed too. She raised both hands and reached out, her fingers grasping like claws.

Kylie stepped back out of the way just as she lunged for her. The woman spun around with a snarl, and made a grab for Britney's tracksuit top. Britney cried out and swung a fist at the woman's mouth, bursting her bottom lip. Blood dripped down her chin and spattered onto the baby's head. The baby thrashed wildly against its restraining harness, seemingly desperate to get at Britney itself, but its arms weren't long enough to reach her. It hissed in frustration.

Mike tried to wrestle Britney from the woman's grip, but she clung on tight, her fist clenched around Britney's tracksuit top. He struck her on the arm with the blade of his hand, but all that did was drag Britney closer to the woman's gnashing teeth. Britney yelled and pushed out with both hands, kicked out at her legs. She snarled and jerked her head forward, then clamped her teeth over Britney's arm. Britney screamed. Blood gushed.

Tom ran forward and grabbed a handful of the woman's hair, then yanked her head back. She came away with a lump of Britney's flesh in her mouth and thrashed her head from side to side trying to free herself. Britney fell to her knees, clutching her arm, blood pumping between her fingers from a gaping hole. Her face was deathly white as she stared at the struggling woman wide-eyed in shock and fear.

Tom dragged the woman away by her hair while Mike knelt down and reached into Britney's backpack. He pulled out one of the designer shirts she had stolen from Sportswear Direct and tied it around her arm, wrapping it around several times in a makeshift bandage.

Tom dragged the woman up to a shop window and smacked her forehead into it, then spun her around and shoved her in the back. She stumbled a few steps, then toppled forward with a sickening crunch. Almost immediately she rolled over and sat up. The baby hung limp from its harness, its head flopped to one side, blood dripping from its ears. The woman bared her teeth and hissed. Tom stared down at her and backed away, horrified at what had happened to the baby. The woman leaned forward and dropped onto her hands and knees, then started to crawl toward him with the baby's limbs dangling lifelessly beneath her.

Tom looked at Mike, his eyes wide and staring. "Let's get the fuck out of here," he shouted, and ran.

4

Smiffy lounged against Meadowside's bronze war memorial statue with his mate Stonker, both of them posing with cans of Special Brew while Johnno took a photo with his phone. Stonker gurned at the camera, displaying his missing front teeth with pride. Smiffy held up the red and yellow football scarf tied around his wrist and clenched his fist.

"Skumfuckers!" he yelled, just before the phone's camera flashed.

Passers by glanced in his direction, then looked away quickly and walked on. Smiffy didn't care what they thought of him. They were nothing. Worse than nothing. Just mindless sheep going about their mundane lives in pointless obscurity, destined to be forgotten the minute they died. Smiffy was a *someone*. He'd built his Skumfuckers firm up from nothing, organised disjointed football yobs and louts into a force to be reckoned with. One to strike fear into the hearts of rival firms. Smiffy had no doubt the Skumfuckers would go down in history one day.

Shefferham United had done them proud that day, winning three-nil against arch-enemies Chelterton FC. The Chelterton Boot Boys, despite all their threats on the Skumfuckers' Facebook page, had been a no-show inside the stadium. Even outside on the streets they hid behind the skirts of an army of coppers like a bunch of frightened schoolgirls as they skipped off back to the train station and went on their way back to their rat-infested home town.

The chant had gone out – CBeebies, who the fuck are you? – but none of the Chelterton Boot Boys took the bait. No doubt they would come up with some lame excuse, but Smiffy knew the truth. The CBeebies had bottled it. And as soon as Smiffy got home he would update the Skumfuckers' Facebook page to let the whole world know about it. But for now he was content to just drink a toast to Shefferham United and celebrate the sound thrashing Chelterton FC had received. The other Skumfuckers had gone home to their wives and kids, but for Smiffy, Stonker and Johnno it was the start of a twelve hour drinking session that wouldn't end until the early hours of the following morning.

Johnno swaggered over, holding his phone out so Smiffy and Stonker could see the photo he had taken of them. Smiffy grunted his approval. Both his and Stonker's huge, bright red pupils made them look like demonic warriors. Stonker drained his Special Brew and crushed the can in one hand. He lobbed it at the war memorial statue and cheered when it bounced off a soldier's head and clattered to the ground. An old woman glared and tutted as she passed.

"Fuck off, you old bag," Stonker shouted.

He took a step toward her with his fist raised. The woman hobbled away muttering something about damn hooligans with no respect for anything.

"Respect is fucking earned," Stonker shouted after her. He cracked open another can of Special Brew and took a long swig.

Smiffy smiled and shook his head. He knew Stonker was only teasing the old woman, but it had certainly put a spring in her step. He took another gulp of his own Special Brew and watched her lose herself in the crowd of shoppers.

Something caught Smiffy's eye, a quick flash of movement in the distance. Someone screamed. Shoppers plodded to a halt and grew silent, looked at each other. Another scream. People craned their necks to see what was happening, then scattered in all directions.

Smiffy climbed onto the war memorial and stretched himself up to see what the fuss was about. People ran by on both sides, wide-eyed and terrified. One woman dragged a young child behind her, the child stumbling as it tried to keep up with her fast pace.

There was some sort of commotion outside the off-license, a lot of pushing and shoving going on. Smiffy saw someone pinned up against the shop window by three men. A woman, judging by her hysterical screams. A young man went to her aid and got dragged to the ground for his troubles. They pounced on him, no doubt for a quick bit of facial reconstruction for interfering with their fun with the woman.

"It's the fucking CBeebies," Smiffy said, pointing. "They must have sneaked off the fucking train at Meadowside."

"The fucking cunts," Johnno said, shaking his head. "That's bang out of fucking order."

Smiffy nodded. Attacking innocent civvies brought hooliganism into disrepute, gave everyone a bad name once the TV news got hold of the story. The Skumfuckers would never do anything like that. The Skumfuckers had honour. They had class. They didn't fight women and kids.

There were five of them as far as Smiffy could tell, and they showed no colours. Not one single football scarf or replica kit amongst them, as if they were ashamed to be associated with Chelterton FC. Unlike Smiffy and his mates, who wore their Shefferham United colours with pride. Yellow replica football shirts, yellow and red Shefferham United scarves around their wrists, and the regulation Skumfuckers camouflage shorts with the secret pockets that were perfect for hiding weapons in.

Two of the Chelterton Boot Boys had a young woman between them. One at the back yanked at her hair and she stumbled back, her arms flailing as she cried out. He pulled her down to her knees, then onto her back, and ripped a handful of hair from her scalp. The one at the front dropped down and copped a feel of her tits while she screamed in agony.

Smiffy's blood boiled. He wasn't having that. Not on his

fucking manor.

"Oi, Chelterton!" Smiffy shouted. He held his arms before his chest in a Celtic cross, his fists clenched, knuckles facing the enemy. "Let's fucking have it then, you cunts!"

"Let's just fucking *do* the bastards," Johnno snarled. He raised his arms and held the same Celtic cross pose as Smiffy. "Oi, you fucking Chelterton cunts!" he yelled. "Skumfuckers are going to fuck you up!"

Stonker steamed into action without a word, his football scarf trailing behind him as he ran. Smiffy knew better than that. He untied the scarf from his own wrist and draped it over the outstretched arms of a bronze soldier for safekeeping. Johnno placed his scarf next to it. He looked at Smiffy and grinned. Smiffy grinned back and nodded.

"Skumfuckers!" they shouted in unison, and following Stonker's lead they ran straight for the two men molesting the young woman.

Stonker had already caught one of them square in the face with his jet-black Doc Martens and had him on the ground. He straddled him and dropped down to his knees, then leaned forward while his calloused fists went to work on the man's face.

Johnno launched a steel-toe-capped boot at the back of the other man's head. It landed with a loud crack and the man slumped forward over the woman's body. Smiffy bent down and grabbed a handful of the man's shirt. He pulled him off the woman and looked down at her. She was unconscious, her dress torn open, her bra pulled down. Her exposed breasts were bloody, covered in scratches.

"You fucking dirty cunt," Smiffy shouted, and lay into the man's face with his boots.

He kicked and stamped, continued venting his rage long after the man lost consciousness. He dropped a Skumfuckers calling card next to him and took out his phone. He crouched down and lined up the viewfinder in his phone's camera to include both the man's mashed up face and the *You've been Skumfucked* gold embossed lettering on the calling card.

This was one to go in the Trophy album on the Skumfuckers' Facebook page, and it had to be perfect. He straightened up and examined the photo, zoomed in to check everything was in focus. He left the calling card where it lay, so it would be the first thing the man saw when he regained consciousness. So there would be no doubt who was responsible for the scars he would carry for the rest of his life.

Johnno and Stonker were gone when Smiffy looked up. He put his phone away and wheeled around to locate them, worried they might be swamped by the remaining Chelterton Boot Boys. But they were both handling themselves well enough, holding up the Skumfucker honour in good style.

Johnno had hold of a man's long, wet, straggly hair and was swinging him around by it. The man stumbled and fell. Johnno was on him in an instant. He raised his boot and stamped down on the back of the man's head, crushing his nose against the wooden flooring. Smiffy could hear the resulting crunch of cartilage from where he was standing. That was another Chelterton Boot Boy who wouldn't forget this day in a hurry.

Stonker had another of them backed up against a shop window, his fists pummelling the man's face. The man just stood there and took it. He didn't flinch, didn't even try to fight back. Smiffy had a bit of grudging respect for that. If it had been Smiffy dishing out the punishment he would've let it go at a few slaps and a bloody nose, then sent the man on his way with his tail between his legs. But Stonker wasn't like that. Once Stonker got the bull by the horns he never let go until the bull was either bloody and unconscious, or the coppers dragged him off. Even then Stonker would go down fighting, take a few coppers with him.

A hand grasped at the back of Smiffy's football shirt. Smiffy spun, raising his fists. He caught a glimpse of a wrinkled, grey-haired face just before he lashed out. His fist struck the old woman in the chin and sent her reeling away in the same direction as the false teeth that flew from her mouth.

Smiffy's eyes widened. He raised his hands, palms facing the old woman, and backed away from her. "Sorry missus, I thought you was a CBeebie."

The old woman hissed like a cat, then lunged at Smiffy with her arms outstretched. Bony fingers curled around his neck and squeezed. Smiffy's eyes bulged in surprise. What the fuck was she doing? She was older than his granny, but she was going to try and take him on? She should be at home, knitting jumpers or whatever the fuck it is old people do, not starting fights with seasoned football veterans.

Johnno cried out in pain, breaking Smiffy's train of thought. A Skumfucker in trouble, something Smiffy couldn't ignore. He didn't want to hurt the old woman any more than he had already, even if she was bat-shit fucking crazy, but he had to get her off him so he could go and help Johnno. He grabbed her wrists and wrenched her hands away from his neck, then stretched them out by her sides. If she was a rival football fan Smiffy would have nutted her in the face, or brought his knee up into her bollocks, but with an old woman he wasn't sure what the protocol was. So he just held her there while she hissed and snarled at him, spittle flying from her mouth.

The old woman's head slumped forward and her gummy mouth slobbered over Smiffy's face. Like she was trying to kiss him or something. Smiffy recoiled in revulsion. He released her wrists and pushed out at her chest. She stumbled back a few paces, then lunged forward again with a screech. Her hands grasped, her gnarled, arthritic fingers clenched like claws around his face.

Smiffy lashed out and punched her in the forehead. He'd had enough of her nonsense, and just wanted her to fuck off out of it. The old woman's head snapped back but she didn't let go. Her fingernails raked down Smiffy's face, tearing through skin. Smiffy cried out and kicked at the old woman's leg. A bone snapped with a loud crack. She toppled over sideways, her body stiff, making no attempt to break her fall, and crashed down. She stared up at Smiffy and hissed, then rolled onto her stomach and snarled as she tried to push herself up.

Smiffy resisted the urge to give the old woman the kicking she deserved and skirted around her, looking for Johnno. He found him nearby, laying into a young boy no more than nine or ten years old.

"What the fuck are you doing?" Smiffy yelled. He grabbed the back of Johnno's football shirt and pulled him away from the boy. "You don't smack a fucking junior."

"The little fucker bit me," Johnno said, turning to Smiffy. He held up an arm. Blood dripped from a ring of tiny incisions surrounded by angry yellow bruising. "The little cunt just fucking lunged at me from behind and fucking bit me. He needs to be taught a fucking lesson not to mess with his elders and betters."

Johnno launched a vicious kick at the boy's chest that landed with a thud and a crack and sent him skidding across the floor. The boy bared his teeth and hissed. Smiffy stared down at him in wonder. The kid didn't look like any of the football firm juniors he had come into contact with before. In his Super Mario T-shirt and green trousers he looked more like an average, everyday kid. A bit wet and bedraggled, scuffed and bruised from his tussle with Johnno, but other than that just a regular kid.

Another hiss came from behind Smiffy and he turned to face it. The old woman crawled toward him, dragging her broken leg behind her. Smiffy exchanged glances with Johnno, who had also turned to look.

"What the fuck is going on?" Johnno asked. "First kids, and now their fucking grannies?"

Smiffy shrugged and shook his head. "Fuck knows, but I reckon we should pull out and get fucked off before the coppers get here. Where's Stonker?"

"He's over there," Johnno said, pointing. He cupped a hand over his mouth and shouted, "Oi Stonker, we're pulling out!"

Stonker turned away from a man he had been kicking and raised his left hand in acknowledgement. He smiled, and swaggered slowly toward Smiffy and Johnno with his fists raised high above his head in victory, his blood-spattered football scarf hanging down from his wrist. He didn't see two men close behind stagger toward him with their hands outstretched.

"Stonker, watch out!" Smiffy yelled.

Stonker spun to face the two men. One of them clawed at his shirt, the other grabbed his arm and bit into it. Stonker cried out and punched one of the men in the face, then kicked out at the other.

"Skumfuckers!" Johnno yelled, running to Stonker's aid.

Smiffy was about to join him when a hand grabbed his right ankle and held him in place. He wheeled around and kicked out with his left leg, struck the old woman on the side of the head. She hissed. He kicked her again, but couldn't get her to release her grip around his ankle.

He crouched down and gripped her index finger, then bent it back until it snapped. He grabbed the next finger and snapped that too. The woman continued hissing. Stonker wondered at this. With two broken fingers she should be screaming in agony, but she didn't seem to fucking care. He reached for the next finger, snapped it, then wrenched his foot out of her hand and stamped on her wrist.

Someone jumped onto Smiffy's back with a high-pitched snarl. Small hands wrapped around his face and clawed at his eyes. Smiffy toppled forward and fell heavily on top of the old woman. She hissed and snarled, and writhed beneath him. Smiffy crawled off her and pushed himself up onto his hands and knees, the small figure still clinging to him, then flung himself back on top of it. He heard something crunch, and the hands fell away from his face. Smiffy rolled over, then scooted his knees up and sprang to his feet. The boy in the Super Mario T-shirt sat up and hissed at him.

"What the fuck is wrong with you?" Smiffy shouted.

He kicked the boy in the head and sent him down for the count. The old woman hissed and dragged herself forward with one hand, her eyes wide and staring. Her gummy mouth opened and closed like a demented fish as she shuffled herself closer. Smiffy shook his head and smiled down at her.

"Well you can fuck off too, you mad old bag," he said. "Or you'll get the same treatment as fucking Mario here."

He turned away, suddenly remembering Stonker was in trouble. Most of the civvies had seen sense and scarpered, leaving behind a dozen or so bloodied and unconscious bodies who weren't quick enough. Smiffy weaved his way around them, heading for where he saw Stonker waving his Stanley Knife around.

Four men surrounded Stonker, all gushing blood from where he had slashed their faces. One lunged from the side. Stonker jerked his knife arm to face the attacker. He slashed across the man's neck and kicked out at his chest with the sole of his boot. The man fell back with a rasping gurgle, arterial blood spurting in a wide arc. Stonker turned when another man sprang forward. The Stanley Knife flashed past outstretched hands, sliced through a wrist and sent

31

more arterial blood spurting. Stonker, silent throughout, grinned like a maniac and grabbed the man's hand. He twisted and pulled, jabbed at tendons and sawed through bones until the hand tore off with a wet snapping sound. He rammed the severed hand into the man's gaping mouth and drove his fist into the man's chin from below, forcing him to bite down on it.

Smiffy watched it all in horror. Stonker had gone too far this time. Way too far. If those men died, which was very likely, Stonker would get life for their murder. And Smiffy would be an accessory to that murder, as well as whatever bollocks the old woman and kid came out with. Smiffy wasn't daft, he knew no judge would take his word over theirs, that the coppers could say anything they wanted and make it stick. He'd be an old man before he got out. If he ever did.

They had to scarper, right now. Get the fuck out of there while there was still time.

But there was no way Smiffy was going to approach Stonker alone when he was in one of his battle rages. Especially now he had his blade out. He'd need Johnno to help him get Stonker under control, and even then it wouldn't be easy. Smiffy looked around, but Johnno was nowhere to be seen. He wasn't the type to bottle it, have it away on his toes when his fellow Skumfuckers were in trouble, so he had to be around somewhere. Smiffy thought about asking Stonker where Johnno had got to, but Stonker was still in mid-rage and unlikely to respond. He was straddling one of the men, his knees in a pool of blood gushing from arms pinned beneath them that had been sliced to ribbons. Stonker's tongue protruded from his mouth in concentration as he carved his name into the man's chest.

Smiffy looked beyond Stonker at some of the bodies littering the floor. Close up, he could tell they weren't just unconscious. They were mangled, a mass of blood and gore. One woman had her stomach torn open, her intestines spilling out. Her arms and legs were a mass of gaping bite wounds, her face forever frozen in a silent scream.

Nearby, a man lay spread-eagled and almost naked on his back surrounded by a pool of blood. His face was bloody and unrecognisable, his nose missing. His left cheek was torn open, his bottom jaw visible through the gaping hole. Both his eyes were gone, just red, blood-filled sockets where they should be. Tatters of red and yellow clothing clung to the edges of a large, gaping wound in his chest. Like the woman, his arms and legs were covered in bites. His left thigh was red-raw, large chunks missing from it.

Snarls came from the distance, from the direction of the nearby entrance. Smiffy turned to look. Dozens of people – men, women and children – lumbered through the doors and headed straight for him. Footsteps came from behind. Smiffy raised his fists and spun to face them. Stonker swaggered toward him dripping blood from a bite wound on his arm. His breath came in short, panting gasps.

"Where the fuck's Johnno got to?" Smiffy asked.

Stonker pointed a shaking finger at the corpse lying by Smiffy's feet.

"Them fucking zombies got him," he said, shaking his head. He raised his injured arm and looked down at it. "They got me too. And you know what that means, right? I'm fucking done for. But no way am I going to turn into one of those cunts." He smiled. "So I'm going to take as many of the bastards with me as I can." He raised the blood-soaked Stanley Knife and held it before him like a dagger.

"Skumfuckers!" he yelled, and ran headlong to meet the approaching crowd.

5

Kylie ran, trying not to listen to the screams all around her. She kept her gaze firmly on the ground, not wanting to know what everyone was screaming at. Quick glimpses from her peripheral vision were more than enough to tell her the crazy woman with the baby wasn't alone; there were dozens more like her, maybe hundreds. Why they were acting like that, or what was wrong with them, didn't matter. All that mattered was to get the fuck out of there.

Kylie glanced over her shoulder. Mike and Britney were starting to fall behind. They had slowed to a walk, Britney's deathly pale face grimacing at each step Mike forced her to make. She slumped against him as he tried to support her.

"Keep going," Tom said to Kylie, "we'll catch you up at the train station." He rushed back to help Mike with Britney. Britney grimaced as Tom lifted her injured arm over his shoulder so he could help Mike support her.

Kylie didn't want to leave them behind, didn't want to be on her own in all this chaos. Hysterical men and women shouted and screamed, ran blindly in all directions. Crazies hissed and snarled, lunged and killed. Kylie tried not to look too closely at the bodies lying on the ground. Tried not to think about what the crazies were doing to them.

"Kylie, for fuck's sake, get going!"

Kylie startled. She hadn't realised Tom, Mike and Britney had got so close. Britney's feet were dragging now, slowing them down even more. Her eyes were open, but her head was slumped to one side as if she were unconscious. Blood seeped through the makeshift bandage.

"Are you okay, Britney?" Kylie asked, walking backwards while she peered into her eyes. Britney's pupils were dilated and unmoving. They didn't react when Kylie waved her hand before them. "What's wrong with her?" she asked Tom.

Tom shook his head slowly. "I don't know."

"We should get an ambulance, I think she's seriously ill."

"Yeah, I know. Get my phone out of my pocket, you'll have to do it while we're walking."

Kylie kept pace with Tom and reached into his tracksuit pocket. She pulled out his phone and prodded the screen. Nothing happened. "What do I do to make it work?" she asked. It was nothing like her mother's phone, with that you just pressed numbers below the screen. Tom's phone was all screen, with just four small buttons at the bottom.

"Give it here," Tom said.

Kylie handed him the phone. When Tom gave her it back she dialled three nines, then put the phone to her ear.

"They're not answering," she said.

"Give it a bit longer, they might be busy."

Kylie walked on, listening to the brrr brrr of the phone with mounting apprehension. What if nobody answered? What if whatever was happening in Meadowside was happening everywhere? She shuddered at the thought. No, it couldn't be that. Tom was right, they were just a bit busy. Probably with the riots in Shefferham. They would get around to answering it soon enough, then an ambulance would be on its way to help Britney.

"Watch out," Tom shouted.

Kylie startled and almost dropped the phone. She had been walking straight toward a woman feasting on a corpse nearby. Kylie backed away, but the woman had already seen her. Her eyes were wild and staring, her face slick with blood and gore. Her mouth gaped open and a piece of bloody meat fell from it. She hissed and pushed herself upright. Then raised her arms and launched herself at Kylie.

"Fuck," Tom shouted. "Kylie, come and get hold of Britney for me."

Kylie gaped at the woman stumbling toward her. Her instincts told her to run, but her legs had turned to jelly.

"Kylie, for fuck's sake, get over here!"

Kylie jumped and spun to face Tom. Tom shook Britney's arm from his shoulder and ran to her. Britney slumped against Mike and he struggled to hold her upright on his own. Kylie hurried over to help Mike, but he had already lowered Britney to the ground when she got there.

Tom punched the woman in the face, then kicked her between the legs. The woman didn't flinch, she just hissed again and made a grab for Tom. Tom darted under her grasping fingers and punched her in the stomach. Again she didn't flinch, didn't double up in pain like any normal person would. Tom darted behind her and kicked out at the back of her knees. She toppled down with another hiss. A kick to the back of the head sent her sprawling forward and she crashed down. She rolled over. Tom stamped down repeatedly on her ankle until bones crunched.

Kylie bent over and retched. Acidic vomit splattered onto her new yellow trainers, but she didn't even notice. She retched again, brought up nothing but bile. She felt the world spinning out of control and reached out for a nearby shop window to steady herself.

"Kylie, come on!" Tom shouted.

Tom was supporting Britney with Mike again. They stumbled past Kylie, dragging Britney between them. Britney's pink tracksuit bottoms were soaked with urine, and left a dripping trail after her. The crazy woman tried to stand and toppled over again when her broken ankle gave way beneath her. She thrashed around, wailing and snarling.

Kylie wiped her mouth with her arm and looked at the screen of Tom's phone. It still said waiting to connect, still made the same brrr brrr sound when she put it to her ear. She prodded the disconnect icon and put the phone in the pocket of her tracksuit bottoms and hurried to catch Tom and Mike up.

Two of Meadowside's security staff ran toward them from the opposite direction, their uniforms splashed with blood. One shouted into a radio, "Moody, where the fuck are you?" They both glanced at Britney slumped between Tom and Mike as they passed, but didn't stop to help.

"Wait," Tom shouted after them, "what's going on?"

"Moody, for fuck's sake come in, man. Where the fuck are you?" the man shouted into his radio. Neither of the security staff stopped running or showed any indication they had heard Tom's question. When they reached the crazy woman rolling around on the floor they skirted around her nervously, then ran on.

"What the fuck?" Tom asked.

Mike shook his head. "Dunno mate, but the sooner we get out of here the better."

They came to a mobility aids shop and Tom told Kylie to go inside and get something to put Britney in so she wouldn't slow them down. Kylie entered the shop and looked around. Tipped over wheelchairs and walking frames littered the floor. A trail of bloody footprints led away from the shop's counter. Kylie didn't want to investigate any further. She bent down to the nearest wheelchair and righted it, then quickly pushed it out of the shop.

Tom and Mike lowered Britney into the wheelchair. She slumped over to one side, her head flopped down on her shoulder.

"She's getting worse," Kylie said, a hint of panic in her voice. "We need to get her to hospital."

"We will," Tom said, "just as soon as we get out of here."

Kylie pushed Britney in the wheelchair while Tom and Mike walked either side of her, ready to defend the two girls from attack. But the crazies had moved on, further into the shopping centre.

Long before they reached the train station exit Kylie knew there would be no way out. The loud moans and snarls coming from that direction made it obvious enough. But Tom insisted they had to see for themselves, just in case. So they crept closer, hugging shop fronts for cover, ready to dart inside at a second's notice.

A large crowd had gathered outside the exit. Bloody fists thumped against the glass, snarling faces smeared mucous over its surface as they tried to bite their way through. They all had vacant, far-away expressions on their faces, like the junkies that hang around the playground on the council estate. Except these were a lot more active than the comatose wasters Kylie was used to seeing.

"What's wrong with you people?" Kylie shouted, close to tears.

The crazies outside became more agitated, their snarls more frantic. Faster, more furious banging on the glass made the doors shake in their surroundings. Someone near the back of the crowd tried to claw his way to the front. Others turned on him and dragged him to the ground, only to be trampled underfoot themselves as more crazies surged forward.

Tom and Mike walked up to the exit doors and looked out. Kylie checked Britney over. Her skin was turning yellow, and sweat dripped from her brow. Kylie felt her forehead, she was burning up. She took out Tom's phone and dialled the emergency services again. This time they were engaged. She hung up and called her home phone, listened to it ring for a full minute. She was about to give up when her mother answered.

"Yeah?"

"Mum, it's me."

Her mother sighed down the phone. "Kylie, where the fuck are you? Your dad's been phoning me all fucking morning wanting to know where you are, he says you didn't turn up for his access time. You know the fucking bastard's blaming me, don't you?"

"Mum, listen –"

"No, you fucking listen, Kylie. He's been calling me all sorts, and I'm not fucking having it. You hear me? I don't fucking care what you've been up to or who with, but if you don't get your arse down to your dad's bedsit right now you're in fucking trouble. Right?"

"Mum, I'm in Meadowside and something's –"

"Hang on Kylie, there's someone at the fucking door. Don't hang up, I'll deal with you in a minute. It had better not be your fucking dad, I can't cope with him turning up today."

Kylie moved the phone away from her ear at the harsh sound of her mother slamming the receiver down on the hallway table. Security chains rattled, bolts drew back. Someone pounded on the door.

"Hold your fucking horses, I'm going as fast as I can," her mother yelled. The door creaked open. "Whatever you're selling I don't want any, so fuck off." The door slammed. Kylie's mother picked up the receiver. "Right then, Kylie, what the fuck are you doing in Meadowside when you're supposed to be with your dad?"

"Mum listen, something's going on and–"

"I said fuck off, I don't want any," her mother yelled. "Hang on a minute, Kylie, I'll just deal with this wanker at the door." The phone's receiver slammed down again. The door creaked open. "Look, you fucking–" The door slammed back on its hinges. Kylie's mother cried out.

"Mum?" Kylie said, her voice trembling. She heard a scuffle, something being knocked over. "MUM?" Her mother screamed for what seemed like an eternity, then fell silent. "MUM!" Kylie yelled, and fell to her knees. Tears rolled down her cheeks.

"Kylie?" Tom said, quietly. He crouched down before her and took the phone from her hand. He listened to it, frowned, then put it in his pocket. He lifted Kylie's chin and stared into her eyes. Kylie threw her arms around him and sobbed into his chest. He held her patiently, rubbing her back until she was able to speak.

"It's ... it's my mum," Kylie blurted out. "I think the crazies got her. Oh god, what are we going to do? They're everywhere."

"I don't know," Tom said. His voice broke up as he spoke, and it brought forth a new round of sobs from Kylie. Tom held her tight.

"Listen," he said eventually, "we're going to get out of this, okay? But we can't stay here. Someone's locked the doors, so we'll need to find another way out."

"But don't you see?" Kylie said. "It's not just here, it's everywhere. There's nowhere left for us to go."

"She's right, man," Mike said. "We're all fucked."

"Shut up, Mike," Tom said. "You're not fucking helping. Listen, Kylie, someone's bound to have called the police by now. They'll be on their way in no time, you'll see. They'll sort it all out when they get here."

Mike grunted. "Yeah well, we'll just have to hope those doors hold out until they get here, otherwise it's fucking game over."

6

Dan Foster didn't know what was wrong with kids today. Too many fizzy drinks and processed foods, probably. All them E numbers and genetically modified horse burgers and what have you sending them all fucking crazy in the head. Feral underclass, the politicians called them. The hooded scourge of decent society, causing chaos and misery wherever they went. Well this bunch of yobs were certainly living up to that stereotype. Vicious little bastards, they should have been strangled at birth.

If Dan was a few years younger he'd sort them out, no fucking problem. He was quite the hard bastard back in his skinhead days, and would have steamed straight in and let his fists and his Doc Marten boots do the talking. Even in his middle age he'd kept himself fit and active down at the gym while his mates grew fat and complacent. But now he had his dodgy heart and his gammy leg to worry about.

The leg he got during the miners' strike, when some bastard copper from down south smashed his kneecap with a truncheon just for calling him a 'fucking pig'. The policeman caused so much damage Dan had needed to have a titanium knee replacement fitted, and it had been almost a year before he could walk properly again. But once he recovered fully from the surgery it hadn't caused him any bother; in fact it came in very handy in a fight, and he thought of it as more of an enhancement than a disability. Smash a metal kneecap into someone's face and they tend to stay down for the duration. Even better, it couldn't be confiscated by police or football ground officials, so it was always there when he needed it.

But as Dan got older the arthritis set in, and now he couldn't even put any weight on that leg without his trusty bulldog-handled walking stick. His dodgy heart was just down to the ravages of time, though his doctor did say all the booze and fags from his younger years hadn't helped.

So when Dan saw three louts setting about an old woman near the wishing fountain all he could do was watch from a distance, hoping one of the people running by would stop to help her. No such luck though. All they cared about was themselves, and fuck everyone else. Things were different in Dan's day. Back then you looked out for each other, stood shoulder to shoulder against the world.

Yeah, he had his fair share of rucks with other tribes. Smelly hippies and punks mostly. And grebo bikers, of course, everyone hated those greasy bastards. He even fought other skinheads sometimes, at football matches when they were on an away day. But batter an old woman? Never. That was something skag-heads did; beating an easy target senseless then robbing their money just so they could pump more poison into their veins.

The youths were pulling the old woman around like a rag doll. She put up a brave fight, cursing like a trooper and lashing out at them with her handbag, but it wasn't long before she was pulled off her feet and the three yobs descended on her.

"Oi, you cunts," Dan shouted, raising his walking stick and shaking it in their direction. "Fuck off out of it and leave her alone."

The three lads took no notice and continued tugging and pawing at the old woman as she screamed and thrashed beneath them. A man in his mid-twenties ran by. There was no way he could have missed the woman's plight or not heard her screams, but he chose to ignore both.

"Fucking help her, you cunt," Dan shouted after him.

But the man continued running without a backwards glance. Dan shook his head and spat in contempt. What the fuck was the world coming to?

The old woman let out a piercing scream.

"Fuck it," Dan said to himself, and hobbled up to the

yobs crouched over the woman. He raised his walking stick and brought it crashing down on the back of the nearest one's skull.

The youth turned his head and looked up at Dan, then hissed through blood-stained teeth. Dan gripped his walking stick in both hands and swung it like a club, hitting the lout in the face with it. The other two looked up and snarled at him, blood dripping from their mouths. Dan glanced down at the old woman between them. Her blouse was torn to shreds, her flat, leathery breasts exposed and bloody. She stared up, her mouth quivering in a silent prayer. Blood pumped from a jagged wound on her neck.

"You fucking animals," Dan roared, and without thinking he lashed out at the nearest yob's head with his gammy leg.

His boot landed on target with a crack and the teenage hooligan fell onto his side, but Dan's knee exploded in pain. He bent down and clutched it while the youth stumbled back to his feet. He hissed and reached out with bloody hands, pawed at Dan's shaved head, and smeared the old woman's blood over his scalp.

Dan recoiled at the slimy touch. He pushed himself upright with a grunt and swung his walking stick up between the kid's legs. He didn't seem to feel any pain, he just stood there hissing like a deranged cat. Dan thrust his hand out palm-first and drove it into his nose. The youth stumbled back with the impact, blood pouring down his face, but again he didn't seem to react to the pain.

More people ran by. Dan watched them with disgust as he staggered back, pain shooting through his leg each time he put any weight on it.

"You fucking cowards," Dan shouted after them.

The teenager shuffled toward him again, fingers grasping. Dan glanced at the old woman. One of the others still crouched over her had his head buried in her chest, making loud slurping sounds. The third glared at Dan with wide, staring, bloodshot eyes. He pushed himself upright and staggered toward Dan, his arms swinging like an ape.

"Come on then, you fucking cunts," Dan growled.

He held his walking stick out before him in both hands and looked from one to the other of the two young men approaching him. As they got closer he jabbed at them with the rubber end of his walking stick. They hissed and snarled in response, and circled him with their arms outstretched. Dan raised the walking stick over his shoulder and thrust it into one of the gaping mouths. Teeth crunched. The kid gagged. Dan pulled the stick out with a wet smack, and swung it at the second kid's head. It landed with a loud crack that sent him stumbling to one side.

The one with the mashed teeth let out a gurgling roar and lurched forward. Fingers curled around Dan's Harrington jacket and pulled him closer. He opened his mouth wide. Blood and teeth dripped down his chin as he moved in to bite.

Dan thrust the walking stick's hard resin bulldog handle back into the youth's mouth, then rammed it down his throat. The kid's already wide eyes bulged even more as he gurgled and choked. His arms flailed, trying to scratch at Dan's face. Then he grabbed the walking stick and tried to wrestle it away. Dan carried on pushing as bloody fingers slipped along the wooden shaft.

The second attacker grabbed Dan's throat from behind and dug his fingernails into his skin. Dan cried out and gave a final push on the walking stick that sent the first kid toppling onto his back. The bulldog handle was slick with blood when it wrenched free. Dan swung the walking stick up over his shoulder to strike the yob holding him. It took three blows before his grip loosened enough to allow Dan to tear himself free and turn to face him. He swung the walking stick's handle into the youth's skull and sent him spinning to the ground.

Almost immediately he rolled over and started to push himself upright. Dan hobbled over to him, using his walking stick for support, wincing at the pain in his gammy leg. The youth was on his hands and knees, looking up at Dan and hissing in anger. Dan slid his hands down the walking stick and raised it like a club.

"Fucking cunt," he shouted, and smashed the bulldog handle down into the young man's skull. "Fucking cunt, fucking cunt, fucking cunt," he yelled again and again as he continued beating the bastard until his hands buckled from beneath him. In his blind rage Dan didn't care what damage he did. He carried on hitting him until his arms ached and he had to come to a panting rest.

Dan lowered his walking stick and leaned on it, his heart racing. His chest constricted, the pain intense. He gritted his teeth and held his breath while he reached into the pocket of his Harrington jacket. With shaking hands he pulled out his Nitrolingual pump and sprayed a couple of puffs onto his tongue, then took deep breaths while he waited for the drug to take effect.

With the worst of the attack over, Dan turned to where the old woman lay. The third hooligan was still crouched over her, tearing through bony flesh with his teeth and hands like a wild animal. Dan limped up to him and raised his walking stick. The wild youth continued his grisly meal, seemingly unaware of Dan's presence. Dan slashed the walking stick down on the back of his head and slamming his face into the woman's chest. He pushed himself up. His head snapped to face Dan. Lumps of bloody flesh dropped from his mouth as he bared his teeth and snarled. Dan looked down at the eviscerated remains of the old woman. His face paled at what he saw.

"You fucking evil cunt!" he roared, and raised the walking stick.

The kid reared up, hissing. Dan struck him between the eyes with the bulldog handle and knocked him onto his back. He hobbled over and rammed the handle into his mouth. Teeth crunched. Dan forced them down his throat, then pulled the stick out and thrust it down again and again into his face. His nose splattered across his face. His lips puffed up and burst open. His cheekbones cracked. All the while, evil red eyes glared up at Dan. Hands grasped at the walking stick, but were too feeble to hold back the blows. Dan smashed the yob's face into a bloody pulp, then turned his attention to the rest of his body until his arms ached so much he couldn't go on any longer.

Dan leaned on his bloody walking stick and panted. He squirted another puff of Nitrolingual onto his tongue and looked around. People were still running by, none of them taking any notice of what Dan had been doing. He stepped in front of one to bar their way.

"What the fuck's going on?" he yelled.

The man skidded to a halt and skirted around Dan without replying. He looked terrified, as did all the others who followed him. Dan looked to where they were running from. He saw a large crowd in the distance, lumbering forward with a stumbling gait, as if they had trouble walking.

Dan stood watching them as they approached. When they came closer he could hear the low murmur of their moans and snarls, could see blood dripping from their hands and faces.

With a final glance at the old woman's corpse, Dan took off his Harrington jacket and laid it over her. He turned and limped away, squirting more Nitrolingual onto his tongue.

7

Special Constable Helen Scott was enjoying her day off browsing in The Lanes, a market-style area on the ground floor of Meadowside set aside for small and local businesses to sell their wares, when she heard the shrill, piercing scream. It came from her left, near one of the entrances to The Lanes. She put down the hand-crafted wooden elephant she had been inspecting, and looked to see what was happening. Nearby shoppers had also stopped to see what the commotion was about, and she had to push through them to see clearly.

A bearded, long-haired, scruffily-dressed man in his mid-forties had a hand around the throat of a young girl from behind, choking her. The girl's eyes bulged in their sockets. Her mouth gaped open as she struggled for breath. The man lifted her from the ground and seemed to sniff the back of her head. The girl's legs kicked out wildly. Her hands flew to her neck and pawed at the fingers grasped around it.

Helen didn't hesitate. "Out of the way, I'm a police officer!" she shouted, barging through the crowd that had gathered to watch.

Despite being only a part time volunteer with the police force – what the regular officers cynically referred to as a hobby bobby – Helen couldn't stand by and do nothing while a child's life was at stake, no matter what her training said the protocol was. She was supposed to call for backup in any cases of violent disorder, and then let the specialists take over. But if she did that, the girl would be dead long before any help arrived.

A youth in a hooded top was filming the attack with his phone, and Helen had to push him out of the way to get closer to the man with the girl. He swore at her and resumed filming. Helen decided she would deal with him later, and confiscate his phone for use as evidence.

"Put her down, right now! You're under arrest!"

The bearded man bared his teeth and growled like a dog. He stared at Helen with wide, piercing, bloodshot eyes and stepped toward her, still holding the girl before him in one hand like a grotesque, struggling puppet. Someone behind him, a woman from one of the nearby stalls Helen had been browsing earlier, grabbed the man's hair and yanked. The man stumbled back, the young girl's body swinging in the air as he flailed his arms. He made an odd hissing sound through his teeth, like a vampire in an old movie.

Helen didn't know what to make of it. The man was either deranged, or high on drugs. Maybe both. Either way, he was a threat not just to the young girl, but to everyone around him. While he was busy struggling against the woman from the market stall, Helen saw her chance and rushed forward. She seized the man's wrist and dug her fingernails into his skin while she supported the girl's weight with her other arm. Helen twisted and pulled, trying to get the man to release his grip around the girl's neck. The girl's face was turning blue, her tongue lolling from her mouth. Helen knew she didn't have much time left to save her.

The man's hair ripped from his scalp. The woman from the market stall cried out and fell back, still clutching a tuft of hair in her fist. The man surged forward into Helen and knocked her off her feet. She struggled back up, using her grip on the man's wrist as a crutch, and jabbed him in the throat with straightened fingers. The man lashed out at Helen and batted her away. She stumbled back, clutching her smarting cheek. Warm blood dripped down through her fingers.

Other shoppers tried to wrestle the man to the ground. One jumped on his back and grabbed him around the neck with both hands. Another pushed him from the front to unbalance him. But with seemingly superhuman strength, the man refused to go down. He hissed and snarled, his head jerking in all directions, his teeth snapping like a feral dog. He bent down and hurled the shopper from his back, then swung the girl like a club at the one who had tried to push him over.

Helen balled a fist and punched the madman in the forehead to put him down for good. He just stared at her and hissed, his wide, bloodshot eyes boring straight into her soul. His lips curled back into a snarl, and for a moment he looked like he was smiling at her. Then his head jerked forward, his mouth wide open. Helen stepped back just in time and his teeth clashed together inches from her face. She lunged forward again and punched him in the solar plexus, then jabbed him in the left kidney. The man roared and staggered back.

Someone, Helen didn't see who, struck the man on the back of the head with a large bronze table lamp. He lurched forward, then spun around, his fingers still squeezed around the girl's neck. The shopper struck him again, on the side of the head, and he toppled over. The girl crashed down, the madman on top of her. He rolled onto his back and hissed.

Three men rushed forward and pinned him down. The youth with the camera phone moved closer to get a shot of his snarling face. Helen went to the girl. She looked limp and lifeless, her eyes staring vacantly. Blood matted her hair, but Helen couldn't tell where it came from. The madman still clutched her around the neck, despite one of the shoppers holding him down punching him repeatedly in the face.

Helen gripped the girl around the waist and tugged her free from the man's grasp. She lay her down gently, then checked her airways were clear and tilted her head back. The girl's chest rose as Helen blew air into her mouth. She checked for a pulse, but couldn't find one. She thumped her in the chest and began compressions. One, two, three. Then blew more air into the girl's lungs.

She looked up at a snarl from the madman, fearing he was loose again. Six people held him now, while two more struggled to secure his hands and feet with leather belts taken from a nearby stall. Helen continued trying to revive the young girl. The youth with the phone crouched before her, filming her attempts.

"What the fuck is wrong with you?" Helen shouted. "For fuck's sake, put it away and do something useful instead."

The youth shrugged, still filming. "Like what?"

Helen shook her head and sighed. She blew air into the girl's lungs, trying to ignore the voyeuristic youth and his camera phone. The girl still wasn't responding, and Helen feared it might already be too late. She tried to calculate how long she had been deprived of oxygen, tried to remember how long the brain could survive without it before being permanently damaged.

"Has anyone phoned an ambulance?" Helen yelled, looking at the small crowd gathered around her.

"I tried to," someone nearby said. It was another teenager in a hooded top, probably a friend of the one filming. "But there wasn't no answer."

"What do you mean no answer?" Helen asked, taking out her own phone. Emergency services always answered within the first three rings, and they had enough operators to handle even the worst of disasters.

Before the hooded youth could reply, more screams came from the entrance to The Lanes. Everyone turned to look. Helen looked down at the still, lifeless young girl and sighed. She closed the girl's eyelids and placed her arms by her sides, then stood up and faced the entrance.

Twelve figures lurched into The Lanes, swinging their arms by their sides as if they had trouble balancing. They came from all walks of life – young, old, fat, thin, both smart and casually dressed. They lunged at shoppers and pulled them off their feet, lashed out with their hands, snapped with their teeth. Shoppers panicked and ran blindly in all directions.

Helen tried to direct them to the far exit, but struggled to make herself heard over their screams. She knew she had to regain order, for their own safety as well as hers, but they were way beyond listening to reason. She found herself swept up by the mob, herded between market stalls that led nowhere, then back the way they had come. Eventually, either through luck or common sense on the part of the leaders, they found the exit and Helen was carried with them back into the main shopping centre.

She looked around, gaping in shock at the dead bodies littering the concourse. While the panicked shoppers scattered, she took out her phone and dialled the emergency services, then stared at the screen in disbelief when she heard an engaged tone. She hung up and called her local police station. That too was engaged. She tried both numbers again, but still got the same engaged tone. In desperation, and going against all protocol, she dialled her commanding officer's direct line.

"Come on, come on," she said as she listened to the dial tone. It rang out to voicemail. Helen swore. "Ma'am, it's SPC Helen Scott. I've tried ringing the station but it's engaged and I can't get through. I'm in Meadowside, and there's some sort of riot in progress. There are multiple fatalities, and I need urgent backup as well as medical assistance. I'm going to liaise with the security staff here, but you can reach me on this number for updates."

Helen put the phone away and looked up. Pale faces stared down at her from the balcony above. "Where's the security office?" she shouted. Nobody replied. "Does anyone know where the security office is?" Helen repeated.

A man raised his hand and pointed diagonally through

the shopping centre. He pointed straight, not down. Helen took that to mean the security office was on the upper floor. She thanked the man and headed for a nearby escalator, planning what she would do once she got there.

8

"For fuck's sake," Mike shouted, banging his fist against the metal shutters covering the entrance to the chemist. Someone inside the shop screamed. Mike bent down to the letterbox slit and peered through it. "Open up, it's an emergency," he shouted.

"Go away, leave me alone," a woman shouted back.

Mike straightened up and punched and kicked the shutters, making them rattle and shake in their frame. "Open this fucking door, right now!"

"Let me try," Tom said. Mike punched the shutter again and stood to one side. Tom took his place and bent down to the letterbox. "Look, missus, our friend is sick. She's been bitten, and now she's unconscious and she's gone a funny colour. We just need something to help her, that's all, then we'll be on our way."

"How do I know you're not one of them?" the woman yelled.

"We're not, come and see for yourself."

"No, you're just trying to trick me. I've called the police, so you'd better get out of here or you'll be in trouble."

Tom sighed. "Look, we just need something for our friend, and then we'll be on our way. You can look through the letterbox if you want, you don't need to open the door. Please. I think she might be dying, you need to help us."

An ice cold shiver ran down Kylie's spine. She glanced at Britney, then looked back at Tom. Was he right? She knew Britney was in a bad way, but could she be dying, like Tom said? She gulped down a lump in her throat. From inside the chemist came the sound of hesitant footsteps making their way to the door.

"No, it's just a trick," the woman said, and the footsteps receded. A door slammed.

"You fucking bitch," Tom yelled, and punched the

shutters. When he turned to Kylie she saw he was crying. "Kylie, I'm–" His eyes widened, staring at something behind her. Kylie spun around and gasped.

A man lumbered toward them, his lips curled back to show blood-stained teeth.

Mike grabbed the wheelchair and pushed it at a run across to the opposite side of the shopping concourse. The man stopped and turned to watch. He took a step toward Mike, then changed his mind and spun back to face Tom and Kylie. He snarled and staggered forward with his hands outstretched.

"Come on," Tom shouted. He grabbed Kylie by the hand and dragged her along, making a wide berth around the man. The man tried to snatch them as they passed, but was left grasping empty air. He hissed in anger as they ran away. Mike kept pace with them on the opposite side of the concourse with the wheelchair, and veered toward Kylie and Tom once he had skirted around the man. They rounded a corner into another concourse, and slowed to a stunned walk when they saw what lay there.

Bodies littered the ground. One man lay on his back with his arms flayed out by his sides. His exposed ribcage glistened red, his internal organs strewn around him. Another had no eyes, and Kylie could see his jawbone showing through a large hole in his cheek.

A young girl, not much older than Kylie, gave out a faint moan as they passed. She clutched a ragged, gaping wound in her chest and looked up at them, pleadingly. Her intestines curled around her fingers as they tried to squeeze their way out of her body. Her face was pale, deathly white, her lips an odd bluish colour. Kylie knew there was nothing they could do for her, and hoped the girl wouldn't suffer too much before she died.

Mothercare's shop-front window was smashed, and muffled screams of agony came from somewhere inside.

Kylie didn't want to think about what might be happening in there. Dozens of crazies milled around inside the shop, knocking things over and fighting amongst themselves. A man locked eyes with Kylie and stumbled up to the broken window with a snarl. The others turned to see what had drawn his attention, then they hissed as one and followed him out of the shop.

Kylie didn't need to wait for Tom to tell her to run. She ran blindly, screaming, desperate to get away from the things she knew would be in hot pursuit. Tom called after her, told her to wait, but she didn't dare stop. She ran on, her heart hammering in her chest like it was trying to burst out.

"Kylie, wait," Tom shouted again.

Kylie blinked back her tears and shook her head. She skidded to a halt. Dozens of crazies crowded around the base of an escalator before her, and she had been running straight for them. Terrified shoppers looked down from above. Someone screamed when one of the crazies stepped onto the escalator. The woman's arms flailed wildly. She lost his balance and fell forward onto her face. Others climbed over her and lashed out at each other over the confined entrance to the escalator. Another stumbled onto the escalator and fell. Then another. And another. They tumbled around together, the escalator's downward motion rolling them over and over.

Kylie felt Tom tugging on her arm and allowed him to pull her away. She sobbed, knowing it was all pointless anyway. They were never going to get away, so they might as well just give in now and get it all over with. Her mother was dead, Britney was probably dying too. The only other person Kylie cared about was Tom, and he was stuck in the same nightmare as her, so why bother going on? Sooner or later the crazies would get them, so why fight it?

Tom pulled her toward a large department store. Kylie

pulled back when she saw blood splashes on its windows, a mangled corpse near the doors. Why would they be any better off in there? She struggled in Tom's grip, desperate to get away, but he held her tight.

"We need to get upstairs," Tom said.

"What?" Kylie stopped struggling and looked into Tom's eyes. "What for?"

"There doesn't seem to be any of them up there yet, otherwise people wouldn't be just staring down at them like that. You saw what they were like on the escalator, I don't think they can work out how to get up there."

"What's wrong with them?" Kylie was close to tears again. She wanted Tom to reach out for her, to hold her tight and tell her everything was going to be okay. But Tom just shrugged and looked away.

"I don't know," he said.

"Probably escaped from a fucking nut-house or something," Mike said.

"What, all these?" Tom said, incredulously. "There's fucking hundreds of them."

"Yeah well, I don't fucking know do I? I doubt anyone does. All I know is we're well and truly fucked."

"You're not fucking helping with talk like that," Tom said, shaking his head. "We just need to get upstairs, then we'll be okay. The coppers will be here to sort it out soon, you'll see."

Mike laughed humourlessly, but didn't say anything else. Tom bundled Kylie through the doors and held them open while Mike pushed Britney through. The department store was in disarray, with scattered garments littering the floor, along with tipped over mannequins wearing the latest fashions. But other than the body near the exit, which Kylie didn't want to look at, there were no people. The shop was deserted, as if there had been a bomb scare and the place had been evacuated. Or everyone had simply vanished.

56

Tom closed the doors and pulled a belt from one of the mannequins, then tied it around the doors' handles to fasten them together. He pulled one of the handles to test its strength, then nodded to Mike.

"Should be okay. Come on, this way," he said, and led them to a lift in the centre of the department store. He pressed the lift's call button, looking around anxiously.

Kylie knew how he felt. Her skin prickled with unease. The shop was too quiet, as if all the crazies were hiding somewhere and watching, waiting for their chance to leap out and pounce. The lift door pinged, making her jump, and slid open with a faint whir.

"Ground floor," a woman's disembodied voice said from the lift, "Ladies' and gentlemen's clothing and accessories."

Mike pushed Britney inside and pressed the first floor button as soon as Tom and Kylie joined him.

"Lift going up," the voice said as the door closed.

"First floor, death and destruction," Mike said.

Tom wheeled on him. "For fuck's sake Mike, pack it in! I mean it this time."

The lift door opened. "First floor, fancy goods, kitchenware and electricals."

Tom stepped out cautiously while Mike held the lift door to stop it closing. Tom looked around, then beckoned for the others to join him. Kylie squeezed past the wheelchair and hurried to his side. The upper level of the shop seemed normal. No dead bodies, no pools of blood, no disarray. Just neat rows of boxes on shelves, and a stack of televisions in the far corner all playing the same music video with the sound turned down low.

Tom walked over to the televisions and crouched down in front of one. He flipped open a panel at the side and changed the channel to BBC News. The screen changed to show shaky aerial footage of a large group of crazies laying siege to a town centre, above a banner reading LATEST:

RIOTS BREAK OUT IN MAJOR YORKSHIRE CITIES, PM TO MAKE A STATEMENT SHORTLY. Tom turned up the volume. A news reporter shouted to be heard over the constant whir of helicopter blades accompanying the scene.

"... which is thought to be instigated by an anarchist group refused permission to carry out anti-austerity demonstrations in the area recently. Copycat riots have now spread to other major cities in Yorkshire. We're looking at large scale looting in progress in Shefferham town centre, with the police seemingly unable or unwilling to contain it. We can see roadblocks on the outskirts of town, but as of yet no riot police have been deployed. There seem to be casualties, we can see several people lying injured, but as of yet there are no ambulance crews in sight."

The video cut to the news room studio, with the scenes from Shefferham town centre continuing in silence on a screen to one side of the newsreader. "Tom Staples reporting live from the scene there," the man said. "We'll keep you updated on new developments as they happen, but right now we're going to Downing Street, where we're expecting a statement from the Prime Minister shortly."

The image switched to a view of Number 10's doorway, where two policemen brandishing semi-automatic rifles stood guard and glared at the camera. After a short pause, the door opened and the Prime Minister walked out to a strobe of camera flashes and a barrage of shouted questions from gathered news reporters. Dozens of microphones were thrust at his face. He held up a hand and smiled, waiting for silence.

"We have all seen the sickening images relayed from Yorkshire today. There is no excuse for violent protests of this kind, and there will be no hiding place for those responsible. These anarchists will be apprehended, and they will feel the full weight of the law."

"Prime Minister," someone off-camera shouted, "can you

comment on the report that South Yorkshire Police are not responding to calls for information?"

The Prime Minister raised a hand. "I would urge all law-abiding citizens to remain in their homes for their own safety until order is reinstated. Social media has been disabled until further notice under emergency regulations brought in by the last government, and IT specialists are searching Twitter and Facebook for the instigators of the copycat disturbances as we speak. I will be looking into whether charges of treason can be brought against those responsible, which carries a mandatory life sentence."

"Prime Minister, what is your response to Labour's claim that you have turned your back on the people of Yorkshire once too often, and that you yourself are responsible for these disturbances?"

"Parliament has been recalled from recess, and I will be tabling measures to declare a state of emergency in The Commons later today. It is the right thing to do, and my government will ensure it is done as quickly as possible. That is all, thank you."

Reporters rushed forward and shouted questions while the Prime Minister retreated back into Number 10. The police officers moved in front of the door and pointed their rifles menacingly. The video cut back to the news room studio.

"The Prime Minister there, outlining steps the government will be taking to deal with this developing situation," the newsreader said. "We'll now go back to Tom Staples for the latest on the riot in Shefferham."

"What the fuck?" Mike said. "He didn't say anything about people being killed and eaten."

"That's because he's a fucking brainless Eton toff," someone said. "He hasn't got a fucking clue what's going on, and never will." Kylie startled and spun around. A crowd had gathered silently behind them, and stood gaping at the

59

television screen. "Fuck knows why people keep voting for useless cunts like that."

The speaker was an old man, who leaned on a blood-stained walking stick. He stood at the front of the crowd, and wore a red, short-sleeved, check-patterned shirt with splashes of blood down it. Blood also spotted his faded denim jeans, which were turned up three inches at the bottom to reveal a pair of large boots. A pair of red braces hung down from his waist. Other than his wrinkled old face he looked a bit like one of the skinhead characters from the movie playing in the cinema. He even had similar tattoos – ACAB and SKINS written on either side of his neck, and bulldogs, skulls and union jacks on his arms.

"Fucking anarchists my arse," the old man continued. "Those cunts out there aren't no fucking crusty anarchists, and they sure as fuck aren't going to just stand around singing protest songs while the coppers crack their fucking heads open."

Kylie had never heard an old man swear like that, and couldn't help smiling. The old man caught her eye and grinned back, displaying crooked yellow teeth.

"All right, darling?" he said, then pointed at Britney. "What's up with your mate there?"

"Um…" Kylie said, her smile fading. She looked at Britney.

"Some fucker bit her," Tom said.

Several people in the crowd gasped and backed away. The old man nodded grimly. "A few tried it with me too," he said, "but they picked the wrong cunt to mess with that time."

"Do you know what's going on?" Tom asked.

The old man shrugged. "No more than you do. Someone said they were zombies, but I reckon that's just a load of bollocks. There's no such fucking thing as zombies. More likely it's the fucking government testing some new weapon on us."

"Why would they do that?" Kylie asked.

"Why wouldn't they? They're all a bunch of corrupt bastards, and they've always had it in for Yorkshire. I wouldn't put anything past them. One thing's certain though, we're on our own here. No fucker's coming to help us."

"So what do we do?" Tom asked.

The old man smiled. "Well the way I see it, we've got two choices. We can either stand around like this and wait for some fucker to eat us, or we can go out there and kill the bastards before they get the chance."

"What?" Kylie said, wide-eyed. "You can't kill people, that's murder."

The old man laughed and shook his head. "And what they're doing isn't? Wake the fuck up, missy, we've got no fucking choice."

"But –"

"No, the guy's right, Kylie," Tom said. "We've got no choice, it's us or them. Besides, it would be self defence, and that's allowed by law. I read about it on the internet once, if someone breaks into your house you're allowed to kill them. It'd be the same thing here."

"And you could do that, could you? Kill someone, I mean?"

Tom shrugged. "If I had to."

"And what about you, Mike?"

Mike frowned. "I reckon we should find somewhere to hide until the coppers get here. Lock ourselves away until it's all over. If we go out killing people we'd be no better than they are, and if we're out here when the coppers come we'd just get arrested along with the whackos."

The old man snorted and shook his head. But before he could say anything further, Britney gave out a rasping moan. All eyes turned to her as she struggled out of the wheelchair.

61

9

"Ow, me head's fucking banging," Britney said, rubbing the back of her head. She looked around, a confused look on her yellow face. "Where the fuck *are* we, and why is everyone looking at me like that?"

"Oh god," Kylie said, rushing up to Britney. She threw her arms around her and hugged her tight. "We thought you were going to die."

"What are you going on about, Kylie?" Britney asked.

Kylie broke the embrace and held Britney at arm's length. She peered into her eyes. "Don't you remember what happened?"

Britney frowned and shook her head. Then startled and craned her neck to look down at her injured arm. She spun around, breaking contact with Kylie. "Oh fuck, that mad woman with the baby! Where is she?"

"Don't worry," Mike said, "she's long gone. But she isn't the only one like that."

"What?" Britney turned to face Mike.

Mike filled her in on everything that had happened since Britney's attack. Her eyes were wide in shock as she took it all in, looking from Mike to the television screen and back again.

"Fucking ... hell," she said, and slumped back down into the wheelchair. "So what do we do now then?"

"We get out there and fucking kill the bastards," the old man said. "If it's right about all the doors being locked, then there's just the ones inside we need to deal with. Should be a piece of piss if we all work together."

Mike wheeled on him. "No we don't, we find somewhere safe to hide until the police get here." There were a few murmurs of agreement from the crowd.

The old man laughed. "Yeah, right. Like that's going to fucking happen. Look at that–" he pointed at the television, showing the scene from Shefferham town centre. "You see any fucking coppers there? The fucking government probably shipped them all out as soon as it started, so they can protect them down in that fucking London of theirs. No fucker's coming to save us, we need to save ourselves."

"And just how do you propose we do that?" a young woman asked.

The old man turned and looked her up and down. He shrugged. "We all get tooled up, then smash their fucking heads in." He raised his blood-stained walking stick. "I've already done a few of the cunts myself, so it's not exactly fucking hard. If we all pull together we'll get it done in no time."

"My god, you're actually serious about this, aren't you?" The woman's face paled. "You can't just take the law into your own–" her voice trailed off when a female metallic voice came over the shopping centre's intercom.

"Attention. This is … um … this is the police. The situation is under control. Please make your way to the second floor immediately. Do not approach any strangers, and do not stop to retrieve any belongings. Once there, make your way quickly but calmly to The House of Fun children's play area situated near the south exit and await further instructions. I repeat. This is the police. The situation is under control …"

"You see?" the woman said when the message started repeating. "The police are here already."

"Under control my fucking arse," the old man said with a scowl.

"Oh, come on! Why would they say it if it wasn't true?"

"Fucking coppers lie all the time, it's part of their job description. You hear any shooting?"

"No, why?" the woman asked.

"Well there you are then. If they're not shooting them fucking cunts out there they haven't got them under control, have they? Stands to fucking reason, it's not like they're going to give themselves up peacefully, is it?"

"They could be using tasers?" Kylie said.

The old man looked at her and frowned. Kylie got the impression he hadn't thought of that. "Yeah well," he said, "fuck the coppers and fuck what they say. I'll take my own chances, thanks. The rest of you can do whatever the fuck you want."

He turned to leave. Several people followed him, talking loudly about what they could use as weapons. Tom was about to join them when Kylie held him back.

"Wait, we should at least go and see what the police have got to say. It can't do any harm, can it? Where was it they said, The House of Fun? Does anyone know where that is?"

"I do," Mike said. His face reddened when Tom looked at him quizzically. He shrugged. "I take my kid brother there sometimes, don't I?"

People started to drift away. Tom stared at the television news. A huge mob of crazies surrounded a corner shop, all banging furiously on its doors and windows. "You're wrong, you know. We need to keep moving, not lock ourselves away. We've done okay so far, haven't we?"

"You call this doing okay?" Mike asked, pointing at Britney. "We've just been lucky, that's all."

Outside on the balcony, someone screamed. Tom ran for the exit while Mike helped Britney out of the wheelchair. Kylie hurried to catch Tom up. He leaned over the balcony, looking down at a huge, snarling crowd of crazies surrounding a nearby escalator. They climbed over each other in a pile of flailing arms and legs to create a swaying tower of flesh six feet high. Those on top clawed their way over and fell, spilling onto the escalator to join the crazies who were already tumbling around there. They crawled over them, taking their place at the head of the queue half way up the steps, where their motion was halted by the downward movement of the escalator beneath them.

"Oh shit," Kylie said. "They're coming up."

Tom nodded, still staring at the crazies on the escalator. "Doesn't look like we'll have long either. We should get out of here while we can."

"Let's go and find those coppers," Kylie said, "and tell them what's happening. They'll know what to do."

10

It took Kylie and the others almost twenty minutes to reach the play area at the opposite side of the sprawling shopping centre. Brightly coloured clown faces smiled down from its boarded over shop front. Above the door, which was painted to look like a cave entrance, was the phrase Welcome to The House of Fun.

A large crowd had gathered outside, with more people standing just inside the doorway. Others were arriving all the time from both directions. They looked bewildered and terrified by what they had witnessed, but were quiet and subdued, as if they had already given up any hope of survival. Some had minor injuries, bruises and scratches or grazed knees from where they had stumbled and fallen. Others were more badly injured, and displayed the same yellow skin-tone as Britney. Kylie looked at each of them in turn, but saw nobody who looked like a police officer. Nobody who seemed to know what they were doing.

An overweight woman in her mid-thirties sat slumped against the balcony. She sobbed to herself, clutching tattered strips of clothing over her scratched breasts. Her face was deathly pale, her eyes red and puffy from crying. Nobody took any notice of her. People either shuffled around her or stepped over her legs, as if she wasn't there.

"So where's all the coppers then?" Tom asked.

Kylie frowned. "I don't know. They must be inside or something?"

Tom grunted and led them closer to the entrance door, pushing his way through the crowd milling around outside. Kylie peered through the doorway. Inside, dozens of yellow-skinned people lay on soft foam play equipment. A young woman with a small first aid box attended them, applying bandages to their wounds. She had angry red scratches on one side of her face, which had scabbed over. Mounted on one wall, a large flat-screen TV silently showed Postman Pat making a delivery to Mrs Goggins.

"Where's the police?" Kylie asked.

The young woman glanced at her and looked away, continued wrapping a bandage around a man's arm. "That would be me," she said quietly.

"You don't look like no copper," Tom said. "Where's the rest of them?"

"I'm off duty. Reinforcements will be here soon, but until then it's just me."

Tom sucked through his teeth. Kylie's heart sank. She had been hoping their ordeal was over, that they'd be rescued. But it looked like they were no better off than they had been before.

"Fuck this," Tom said, turning away. "That old geezer was right, we're on our own here."

"No, wait," the police woman said. "We need to stick together. We're perfectly safe up here, we just need to wait for help to arrive."

Tom turned back to the woman and shook his head, frowning. "Not for much longer we're not. There's loads of them making their way up the escalator right now, we've seen them."

People in the crowd by the door gasped and looked around fearfully. The police woman looked at Tom, wide-eyed.

"Where?" she asked.

"Near the fountain," Kylie said.

The police woman held her hands together over her mouth, as if she were praying, and sighed. "Okay, thanks for telling me." She brushed past Kylie and forced her way out onto the balcony. "Okay, listen up everyone," she shouted, "I need you all to move inside. It will be a bit cramped, so move as far to the back wall as you can. Anyone who is injured, wait by the mats at the front for treatment.

The rest of you, find space where you can."

Kylie was about to enter when Tom pulled her to one side. "We'll be safer out here," he said.

"What?" Kylie resisted as people streamed past her into the play area. It was obvious they wouldn't all fit, so any delay just increased their chances of being left out to fend for themselves.

"Think about it," Tom said. "Out here we can move fast if we need to. In there, we'd be stuck in one place. If they get in, there'd be nowhere for us to go."

"But she said the police are on their way, we just need to wait."

Tom shook his head. "Kylie, you saw the news. They're not coming. Our best bet is to find that old geezer and the others, get something to defend ourselves with if we have to. But we need to keep moving, not lock ourselves away and get trapped."

"We're staying," Mike said. Tom turned to face him. Mike shrugged. "Britney's injured, she needs first aid. In there's the only place she'll get it. I get what you're saying, but if we all keep quiet we should be okay in there. The windows are boarded up, so they won't even know we're in there."

"You think those people are capable of being quiet? Mate, look at them. They're in shock, they'll panic at the slightest sound. And it'll only take one to set them all off."

"Yeah well, maybe. But we're still staying. You should, too. You're not fucking Rambo, no matter how much you might think you are."

"Fuck off, Mike, you know I'm right. If those nutters get through that door with you all inside you've got no chance. At least out here we can run. We've done okay so far, haven't we?"

"We were lucky, that's all," Mike said, shaking his head. "Doesn't mean a fucking thing."

"Britney?"

Britney looked down, avoiding Tom's questioning gaze.

"Well there's your answer," Mike said. "You should stay too, Kylie. Go with Tom and he'll just get you killed."

Tom looked at Kylie. Kylie looked away, torn between what to do. She knew what Tom was saying made a lot of sense, but she was tired of running. She looked to the play area entrance, watched people pushing their way through in a panic. The police woman tried to herd them through one at a time, but was fighting a losing battle as they all tried to squeeze through the narrow entrance together. The way they squabbled amongst themselves reminded her of the way the crazies all tried to crowd onto the escalator at once. She didn't fancy the idea of being squashed up against that many people in a confined space for who knows how long, but was the alternative any better? Running for her life, with nowhere to run to, no hope of rescue?

"We're pretty much fucked either way, aren't we?" Kylie said. She felt her eyes welling up, and blinked away the tears.

"Kylie, I can keep you safe," Tom said. "I promise."

Kylie sighed. She turned to Mike. "You'll look after Britney, won't you?"

"You're not fucking serious?" Mike said, his eyes wide.

Kylie hugged Britney. "I'll see you later," she said, and turned and walked away before she could change her mind.

11

Greg Thorndyke knew there were too many people in the lift already, but pressed up tight against the glass at the far side there was nothing he could do about it. He tried pushing them back, but the sheer weight of all the people trying to squeeze themselves into the already full to capacity space made it a pointless battle. He yelled at them to get out, to use one of the escalators instead, but nobody was prepared to listen to logic or reason.

In their blind panic, all anyone cared about was securing their place inside at any cost. They punched and kicked those near the entrance, dragged them out onto the concourse, and took their place inside the lift; only to be attacked themselves by others trying to get in. Someone jabbed at the control buttons constantly, as if that could somehow magically bypass the door's safety mechanism and force it to close. But with the baying crowd in the doorway, the door barely moved an inch before it sprang back open.

Greg's breath came in wheezing gasps. He could feel an asthma attack coming on, but with his arms pinned by his sides he knew there was no way he could retrieve the inhaler from his pocket. All the people crushed up against him were faring no better. One of them, an old woman in her sixties, looked like she was unconscious. Her head had flopped to one side, her eyes had rolled up in their sockets so only the whites were visible. Greg couldn't tell if she was breathing or not, and knew there would be nothing he could do for her either way. All he could do was stand there, squashed up against the glass, and hope for the best.

Greg turned his head, the only part of his body he could still move, and stared out, wishing he could be out there in all that free space. Wishing he was fit enough to take the stairs instead of relying on lifts. Wishing he could afford to heat his home so he wouldn't need to spend all day in the shopping centre just to stay warm. Wishing, more than anything, that he was somewhere else, away from all this madness.

He could see the killers approaching from the distance, no doubt attracted by the commotion everyone was making inside the lift. Others must have seen them too, because they started screaming and shouting, their terror soon spreading to everyone else around them. Greg felt himself being crushed as more people tried to cram themselves into the lift. All the while, the killers shambled closer, swinging their arms before them like apes. A huge army of them, descending on the area like cannibalistic locusts, their murderous intent plain on their snarling faces.

Like most people still alive, Greg hadn't seen one close up before. Other than their wide, staring eyes, their gaping mouths, and their stumbling gait, he was surprised how ordinary they looked. They were nothing like the crazed killers portrayed in fiction. Men and women of all ages were in their ranks. Children, too. Most were smartly dressed, though some were covered in so much blood it was hard to tell what they were wearing.

The screams grew louder and more frantic when the killers started pounding on the glass walls of the lift. A man directly in front of Greg smeared bloody mucous across the surface as he tried to bite his way through. Greg closed his eyes and turned his head away. He mumbled a prayer to himself that he knew would never be answered.

The pressure around Greg seemed to ease a little, and he found it easier to take wheezing breaths. He still needed his inhaler, but at least what little oxygen he could get into his lungs wasn't being squeezed out by the crush of people around him. He tried to move his arm so he could reach into his pocket, but the pressure hadn't eased that much yet. He opened his eyes and peered past the old woman, past the crowd of bodies holding her upright. People were no longer fighting to get inside the lift. They were fighting to get out, and running in all directions when they managed it.

Greg felt a slight glimmer of hope. If enough of them left, the door would be able to close fully and whoever remained could be transported to the upper floor, where the police said it was safe from the killers. Bodies peeled away from the entrance like layers of skin from an onion, allowing those inside to spread out. With nobody to hold her upright, the old woman fell to her knees, then toppled over. Greg took out his inhaler and puffed it into his mouth, inhaled the salbutamol with relief. The lift door closed, painfully slowly.

Then one of the killers stumbled into the opening. Everyone screamed and backed away as he lunged forward to attack. He grabbed a woman by the hair and pulled her head to one side, then bore down on her neck with his gaping mouth. He jerked his head back as he bit into her, and ripped free a chunk of bloody flesh. She screamed while he chewed it with relish.

More killers surged into the lift, hissing and snarling, reaching out with claw-like hands to grab at men and women as they cowered before them, unable to retreat any further. Greg felt his bowels loosen, but was powerless to do anything about it. He could tell from the smell in the lift he wasn't the only one this had happened to, but things like that didn't matter when everyone around him was being torn apart, the glass walls filling up with a thin sheen of spurting arterial blood.

In desperation as the killers made their way toward him, Greg pushed a young woman into their outstretched arms and bolted for a corner of the lift. He lay down and drew dead, mangled bodies around himself, tried to stop his own body from shaking as he listened to the young woman's screams of agony.

When the screaming stopped, all Greg could hear was the killers' laboured breath, the sickening sound of them feasting on those they had killed. He could feel the corpses around him juddering as first the clothes, then the flesh was torn from their bodies. He knew it wouldn't be long until he was discovered. He hoped his death would be quick and painless, but he knew deep down that it would be anything but.

12

Kylie flinched at the way Tom swung the golf club in Sportswear Direct. She imagined its solid steel alloy head shattering through someone's skull, spilling their brains. She shivered involuntarily at the thought, and hoped Tom would never need to use it. Or if he did, which seemed increasingly likely, she would have time to look away first.

"Here, take this," Tom said, holding the golf club out to her.

Kylie shook her head and backed away, her palms raised. "I don't want it."

"You might need it."

"I won't. I wouldn't be able to use it on someone anyway, no matter what they did."

Tom stared into her eyes and frowned. After a few seconds he lowered the golf club and turned away. "Okay girl, but stay close to me, yeah? If any of those fuckers get too close I'll sort them out for you. Now let's go."

"Why don't we just stay here? We could hide in the changing rooms or something until it's all over."

"Kylie, we've been through this already. We need to keep moving, so we don't get ourselves trapped. Just stay close to me and you'll be all right, I promise."

The fluorescent lights in the shop popped and hummed, then went out, plunging the shop into darkness. Kylie fumbled for Tom's hand and clutched it. The lights in the rest of the shopping centre had also gone out, causing a chorus of hisses and blood-curdling shrieks from the crazies on the floor below. Kylie held her breath for what seemed like an eternity, trying to make out shapes in the pitch darkness, terrified at the prospect of fleeing in the dark from killers she couldn't even see.

Dim lights flickered on outside the shop. Kylie looked up and sighed in relief. She turned to Tom and sought out his face in the gloomy light, just a silhouette in the faint glow coming from the shopping centre concourse. They waited a minute to see if the shop's own lights would come back on, and when they didn't Tom led Kylie to the exit, cautiously holding the golf club out before him so they wouldn't bump into anything in the dark.

They walked down the concourse together, trying not to listen to the screams coming from the ground floor below, knowing there was nothing they could do to help anyone still trapped down there. Tom glanced fearfully at each shop entrance they passed, as if he expected someone to leap out at any moment. He said he wanted to check on the situation at the escalator, but Kylie just wanted to get as far away from there as possible. She knew it was only a matter of time before the crazies spilled over the top and continued their rampage across the upper floor. It was all hopeless, they should have stayed at The House of Fun. But it was too late to change her mind now. The play area would stay firmly locked until the police arrived. If they ever did.

Writhing, snarling bodies almost completely covered the escalator steps. Kylie looked down from the balcony as they crawled over each other, no longer encumbered by the escalator's movement. The escalator itself lay still, switched off with the main lights to conserve power for the emergency generator.

Kylie was about to turn and run when Tom pointed out a group of four men clutching an assortment of garden tools nearby. He shouted out to them, then pointed frantically at the escalator. They rushed to the balcony to see for themselves, then ran to the escalator just as the first of the crazies spilled over the top.

A snarling woman struggled to her feet as more crazies made their way up the escalator behind her. One of the men swung a shovel at her face and knocked her down onto her back. Another held her in place with a garden rake while

75

he positioned the shovel over her neck and stamped down on its blade. Blood spurted up the shovel. The woman continued struggling. The man stamped again and severed her spinal cord. He twisted the shovel's shaft and wrenched it free, then turned and swung it at another crazy who approached him from behind.

The other two men stood by the escalator. One repeatedly swung a long-handled axe down into the crazies as they reached the top, hacking through limbs, cleaving through skulls and torsos, while the other used a garden hoe like a jouster's lance to push crazies back down when they reared up. The first two men joined them, then all four took turns lashing out at the seemingly endless stream of crazies making their way up the escalator, crawling over the corpses of their fallen comrades like flies over roadkill.

Kylie watched with mounting fear as the crazies tossed severed limbs in all directions in their haste to reach the top, only to fall victim to the man's axe or get batted in the face by a shovel or garden hoe that sent them tumbling back down the escalator. She gripped Tom's hand tightly.

"They won't be able to keep that up forever," Tom said. "What we need to do is block off all the routes upstairs."

"How?" Kylie asked. She wanted to look at Tom, question him further, but her eyes were firmly rooted to the grisly scene at the escalator.

"Dunno. Whatever we can find, I guess. And we need to be quick too, because that's not the only way up here we need to worry about."

The man's axe sliced down into a crazy's back with a wet thud and a crunch of bones. He tugged on the axe handle, but it was stuck fast in the crazy's ribcage, and all he succeeded in doing was to drag the crazy closer to him. The crazy reached out and grabbed the man's ankle. He cried out and raised a boot to stamp down on the crazy's wrist. Bones splintered and the hand fell away. He bent down and struggled to free his axe while the crazy snapped his teeth at the man's feet. The man with the shovel stepped forward and kicked the crazy in the face, lashed out with the shovel, then bent down to help pull out the axe.

"Kylie, wait here," Tom said.

Kylie finally managed to tear her eyes away from the carnage on the escalator and look at Tom. "What? Where are you going?"

"To see if I can find something to block the escalator off with. Here, take this." He held out the golf club, and Kylie took it without thinking. She held it upright before her with both hands and turned back to the escalator. "I won't be long," Tom said, "but if any of those fuckers break through just leg it, don't wait for me. Head for the toilets and lock yourself into a cubicle, I'll come and find you when I can."

Kylie watched Tom sprint for a nearby DIY shop, and suddenly felt very alone and very vulnerable. A golf club would be no defence against hordes of crazies. If the combined might of four men with sharp garden tools couldn't hold them at bay what hope would she have on her own?

"Tom, wait," she shouted, and ran after him.

The man with the garden rake spun to face Tom and cried out. He swung the rake over his shoulder like a very long baseball bat, ready to strike, with vicious-looking sharp prongs facing Tom.

Tom skidded to a halt and raised his hands. "Wait, I'm normal," he shouted.

The man stared at Tom wide eyed for several seconds, the rake still held in a striking pose, then relaxed. "Fucking hell," he said, "I fair near shat meself then, kid. I thought you were one of them fucking zombies."

"Nah mate, we're cool. So's she," Tom added quickly when the man spun to face Kylie. "Look mate, we need to barricade the stairs, there's too many of them fuckers coming up for you to deal with them all like that."

The man frowned, then nodded. "Yeah. Yeah, probably. Good thinking. Oi Dave, here a minute."

The man with the garden hoe looked around. "What?"

"I'm gonna go and get some shit to block the stairs off, you guys be okay while I'm gone?"

Dave looked at the escalator, which was slick with blood and gore, acting as a lubricant to slow the crazies' ascent. Unable to find purchase, they slipped and slid back down, crawling forward slowly like babies on a greased treadmill. Any that reached the top were hacked into pieces with the axe and then sent skidding back down with the shovel.

"Yeah, good idea. Don't be too long though."

Tom and Kylie headed for the DIY shop. The man with the rake followed them, and when he saw where they were going he told them to get some hammers and nails and meet him in the furniture shop a few doors down. When they got there he was already pushing a heavy oak dining table toward the exit.

"Give us a hand with this," he said.

Tom gave Kylie the bag with the nails and hammers, and helped the man carry the table out of the shop and back to the escalator. They put it down and tipped it onto its side, with the legs facing away from the escalator. The man with the axe continued slashing at the crazies while the others pushed the table closer, then jumped out of the way just before it slid into place to block off the escalator. They held the table in place while Tom and Kylie nailed its legs to the wooden flooring, then ran back to the furniture shop.

When they returned, two carried another matching oak table between them, while the others pushed a trolley containing a large, heavy-looking stone garden statue. They hefted the statue over the table blocking off the escalator and dropped it onto the crazies below. Bones crunched as it tumbled down. Crazies hissed as they were bowled over.

Kylie ran to the balcony and watched the statue tumble down the escalator, leaving behind a trail of mangled bodies sliding down after it. When she looked back, the men were lifting the new table over. She expected them to toss it down like they had with the statue, but instead they held it there, resting on the escalator's handrails with two of its legs flush against the underside of the first table. She saw Tom hammering a nail into one of the legs and hurried to secure the other leg herself.

"We need to sort the other escalators out too," Tom said after they finished. "And the stairs." The man with the axe nodded, his eyes wide as if he hadn't considered any of the other routes upstairs. "Then there's the big shops that use both floors, I reckon it'd be easiest to just pull down the shutters on those."

"Yeah. Yeah, good thinking, kid. You do the shutters, we'll sort out the rest. There's other groups fighting back, I'll let them know what to do too. Stay safe, yeah? You'd better get yourselves some better weapons though, that golf club of yours won't be much use." He looked down at his bloody axe and smiled. "You want something like this instead."

Tom's face paled when he looked at the axe, but he nodded nonetheless. "Yeah. Yeah, you're right."

After the men left, Tom and Kylie looked down over the balcony. Crazies were already starting to clamber over the statue lying at the foot of the escalator. Tom pulled Kylie away, back into the DIY shop.

"Go and get me a few rolls of gaffer tape," he said when they walked through the door.

Tom wandered further into the shop while Kylie looked around for the adhesives aisle and located the gaffer tape on its shelves. She scooped up a handful of rolls and headed in the direction she had seen Tom go, near the back of the shop. When she found him he was spinning a broom handle around like a giant cheerleader's baton. On a workbench nearby lay a woodcutter's axe and a large carving knife with a twelve inch serrated blade.

"I found them," Kylie said, putting the rolls of gaffer tape down on the workbench.

Tom nodded, then picked up the axe and held its short wooden handle overlapping the end of the broom handle. "Wrap some tape around these for me."

Kylie picked up a roll of gaffer tape and removed its cellophane packaging with her teeth. She pulled out a long strip and wound it around the axe, securing it to the broom handle. Tom took the roll from her and finished the job, wrapping it around the full length of the axe's handle several times until it was completely covered. He wiggled the axe's blade, then seemingly satisfied it was securely attached he swished it through the air. He picked up the carving knife and held it in place at the opposite end of the broom handle while Kylie wrapped more gaffer tape around it.

Kylie looked at the finished weapon while Tom practiced with it. She had seen something very similar in the Armouries Museum in Leeds on a school trip, and guessed that was where Tom had got the idea from. She couldn't remember what it was called, but it looked deadly.

"We need to make something for you too," Tom said, putting the weapon down on the workbench.

Kylie nodded. She still didn't know if she would be able to use anything like that herself, but she didn't want to be left defenceless against the crazies. Tom handed her the golf club and she held it grimly while he grabbed another carving knife and taped it to the club's head so it stuck out like the grim reaper's scythe.

Tom downloaded the Meadowside App on his phone, and Kylie peered over his shoulder while he consulted a list of shops displayed by category. He narrowed it down to major stores only, and brought up a map showing a suggested shopping route with each store marked with a red dot.

"We're here," he said, pointing at the DIY shop on the map, "so it looks like House of Fraser is the nearest. We'll start there and work our way round."

Kylie nodded and they left the shop together. She looked over the balcony as they passed the escalator, and saw crazies slipping and sliding on the blood-drenched steps. Others were climbing over them, just as they had done when the escalator was moving. She hoped the tables at the top would stop them from spilling over onto the upper floor, but that seemed unlikely. Once the top of the escalator was full of writhing bodies again they would be able to climb over easily. She pointed this out to Tom, but he told her not to worry about it.

"It'll take them hours to get that high," he said. "With a bit of luck they'll just give up, but if they don't we can throw another statue down at them."

Kylie nodded, hoping it would be that easy.

When they reached House of Fraser Tom reached up with the broom handle and hooked the corner of the axe onto the rolled up shutters above the door. He pulled them down and Kylie crouched down to slide bolts into place to hold them secure.

"We need some padlocks for the bolts," Kylie said.

Tom was reaching up, trying to hook the shutters over the display window. He shook his head without looking down. "They'll be okay as they are, we need to stop people getting out, not getting in."

"What if there's someone trapped in there?"

Tom grunted as he pulled down the shutter. "They would have come out when they heard that copper." He bent down and fastened one of the bolts while Kylie walked to the opposite side and fastened the other. "Don't worry about anyone else, we've got enough to deal with ourselves."

"But what about the people still trapped down there?"

Tom didn't reply. He shook his head and looked down at his phone. "Come on, let's go. The next one's down this way."

They had to cross an intersection to reach Marks and Spencer, where the upper floor branched off in three different directions. Tom checked the map on his phone and took them right. They passed a lift shaft, the lift itself stuck on the ground floor. The remains of eviscerated bodies lay strewn around its open door, the glass walls awash with blood. But of the crazies who were responsible there was no sign until they rounded another corner into another section of the shopping centre.

They heard the shouting first, and it took Kylie a few seconds to locate where it was coming from. She looked down over the balcony, saw dozens of crazies crowded around the opening to a stairway. The shouting came from somewhere out of sight, but could only be from the stairway itself.

"Fuck," Tom said, running toward the sound. "Come on."

Kylie wanted to get away from there, but she couldn't leave on her own, so she followed Tom with the golf club held grimly before her. They reached the stairway just as three men backed out of it. Kylie couldn't be sure, they were unrecognisable under a thick coating of blood and gore, but from the garden tools they carried she assumed they were the same men they had met at the escalator. One had obviously fallen victim to the crazies since then, most likely on the stairway. She felt sick to her stomach at the thought of what had happened to him.

Two of the men held a garden rake horizontally between them across the stairway opening, trying to hold back the snarling crazies crowded up against it, while the other hacked and slashed with an axe. Tom rushed up to them, lifting his own axe over his shoulder. He swung it down into the crazies again and again, slicing through outstretched arms, shattering through skulls, showering himself in spurts of blood.

But the crazies were too strong, too numerous to be held back. Inch by inch, the men with the rake were pushed back as more crazies swarmed up the stairs and joined in the scrum. Tom and the other man were forced to step back so they could maintain their attack on the front line, but for every crazy that fell, more climbed over their bodies and took their place.

The gap between the stairway and the garden rake increased under the combined weight of the crazies, until it was big enough for some to squeeze out either side. Tom jabbed one in the eye with the carving knife taped to the end of his broom handle, then ripped it out and swung the axe at the opposite end into the face of another. The man with the axe backed away in Kylie's direction, slashing wildly at the crazies approaching him.

One of the men with the rake stumbled and fell. Crazies swarmed over him and he screamed pitifully while the other man wrenched the rake away and swung it at the legs of the crazies before him, bowling them over like snarling skittles. The fallen man fell silent. More crazies swarmed out of the stairway, blocking Kylie's view of Tom. She could hear him shouting, telling her to get the fuck out of there, but she couldn't see where he was. All she could see were the crazies heading straight for her, the man slashing at them with his axe doing little to halt their progress.

The man with the rake found himself surrounded by crazies too close for him to bat away. One bit into his cheek and shook its head like a dog until the flesh ripped free. The man screamed and fell to his knees, crazies falling with him as they bit into his shoulders, neck and back. One chewed off the fingers of the hands he held before him in a futile attempt to protect himself. Another grabbed his hair and pulled him down. He carried on screaming as they swarmed over him, fighting amongst themselves for prime position around his body, until he gave out a final gurgling cry and lay silent while they tore him apart.

"Run!" the man with the axe shouted.

Kylie blinked, unable to take her eyes off the crazies fighting over the remains of the man with the rake. One held up a severed arm triumphantly, dripping blood from a ragged tear where it had been ripped from its socket. Another tried to take it from him and they lashed out at each other with claw-like fingers.

"Tom!" Kylie yelled. She backed away as the crazies got closer. "Tom! Where are you?"

The man with the axe glanced over his shoulder at Kylie. "Fucking run!" he shouted.

His momentary break in concentration cost him his life. A crazy lurched forward and grabbed the axe handle just as he was about to swing it. He struggled to wrench it free while others advanced on him. They pulled at his clothes, yanked at his hair. He kicked out at their legs and tried to twist himself free, but there were too many.

"Run!" he shouted again as they pulled him to the ground.

Kylie backed away, tears streaming down her face while she watched the crazies' feeding frenzy. Her legs felt like jelly, unable to support her. She reached out for the balcony to steady herself as she continued backpedalling, then turned and ran when the crazies turned their attention to her. She could hear them lumbering after her, dozens of heavy footsteps clumping over the wooden flooring, but didn't dare look to see how close they were. They hissed and snarled after her, as if they were commanding her to stop.

She tripped and fell, then landed heavily on her hands and knees. The golf club clattered away from her. She scrabbled after it and grabbed it in one hand, then stumbled to her feet and swung it at one of the crazies that was only a few feet away from her. The blade on the end of the golf club sliced into an outstretched arm, but didn't slow the crazy's approach. He snarled and reached out for her, blood pumping from the wound. Kylie slashed the blade down into his face, cutting through his top lip and into his mouth. He gurgled, blood gushing from his mouth as Kylie ripped the blade free and turned to run.

Before she could take a step, the man grabbed the back of Kylie's tracksuit top and held her in place at arm's length. Kylie twisted in his grip and lashed out with the golf club, felt the jarring impact in her wrist as it struck home and punctured the man's lung. She tugged it back and felt the blade tearing through his flesh as she struggled to free herself. The man clung on triumphantly, defiantly, blood pouring down his side, his breath coming in a gurgling rasp.

Kylie cried out when she saw how close the other crazies were, and renewed her frenzied attempt to escape the man's clutches. She stamped down on his foot and hit him in the side of the head with the golf club. It was only when the other crazies arrived and attacked him that he let go of Kylie. She stumbled and fell forward, released unexpectedly from the force she had been struggling against. She rolled over and looked up. Snarling crazies lunged forward with their hands outstretched, their bloodshot eyes wide and staring, their mouths open and ready to bite down on her. Kylie could smell the fresh kills on their breath as they descended on her. She curled herself into a ball and sobbed into her hands while she waited for them to tear her apart.

13

Rough hands dug into Kylie's back and tugged at her clothing. The crazies snarled and hissed, lashed out at each other as they fought over her. Sharp fingernails raked over her arms, burning them in searing pain. Kylie screamed and clutched her face tighter, tucked her knees under her elbows. A crazy balled its fists around her hair and pulled back savagely, dragging Kylie across the wooden flooring, her body rigid and unresponsive. Hair tore from her scalp with a ripping sound. Kylie closed her eyes and screwed her face up in agony.

Somewhere in the distance she heard a scooter being revved, like the one Dave Sugden had stolen once and taken everyone for a ride around the council estate on before he set fire to it in the middle of the playground. But that couldn't be right. They didn't allow motorcycles in the Meadowside Shopping Centre, and all the doors were locked so nobody could have brought one in. It had to be her imagination, her mind playing tricks on her. And yet she could still hear the scooter, drowning out the snarls of the crazies as it came closer, the roar of its engine becoming louder and louder, until it was almost on top of her.

Something wet and warm splashed over Kylie's arms. Something small and light hit the back of her head with a soft thud, then fell away. Something heavy slumped on top of her and crushed the breath from her lungs. Kylie squirmed beneath it while the scooter circled her, its two-stroke engine howling in protest. Then with a final rev, the scooter's engine idled to a steady put-put-put. The dead weight was dragged from her. A hand grasped her wrist. Kylie whimpered and struggled as her hand was pulled away from her face. A crazy stood over her, grinning down. Drenched in dripping blood, he held a chainsaw by his side in one hand.

"Are you bit?" the crazy asked. Kylie cowered away, struggling against his grip. "Are you fucking bit?" the crazy shouted. He released Kylie's wrist and raised the chainsaw. Its spinning blades flicked blood into Kylie's face as it moved closer.

"No!" Kylie shouted, covering her face with her hands again. "No I haven't!"

The crazy lowered the chainsaw and grunted. He held out a hand to her. "I'm Smiffy," he said. "What's your name, kid?"

Kylie flinched and shuffled herself away from the man. She realised she was lying in a huge pool of blood, and sat up quickly. The scattered remains of dismembered and decapitated crazies lay all around her. She looked up at the man standing before her, who was still holding out a hand to help her up. Piercing white eyes stood out from his blood-drenched face. Small patches of yellow could be seen on his dark red shirt. He seemed to be wearing shorts, but from all the blood and gore that covered them it was difficult to make out where the shorts ended and his legs began. She clasped the man's hand and allowed him to pull her upright.

"What's your name, kid?" the man – Smiffy – said again.

Kylie felt her knees buckle. Smiffy grabbed her around the waist and held her upright.

"Tom," Kylie said quietly, staring at a severed arm by her feet.

"You what?" Smiffy asked.

Kylie stared into Smiffy's eyes. "Where's Tom?"

"Who's Tom?"

"He's my ... my boyfriend."

Smiffy frowned, then shook his head. "Sorry kid, there was just you when I got here. The zombies must have got him."

"Zombies?" Kylie had heard several people refer to them

as zombies now. Was that really what they were? Had they killed Tom? Eaten him? Kylie didn't want to accept that. He must have got away, killed them with his axe. But why hadn't he returned for her when she was in trouble? Tom wouldn't have just left her to die like that.

"Yeah, zombies. Fucking mental or what? But that's what they are, all right. Shoot them in the fucking head, yeah? Like in the movies, except we ain't got no fucking guns like them Yank bastards in the movies." Smiffy raised the chainsaw and smiled. "So we need to use shit like this, yeah? Fucking smart or what? You just shove it in their faces and it rips them to fucking bits. You were lucky I needed some extra fuel for it, otherwise I wouldn't have been up here getting some when I heard you shouting. What I wouldn't have give to have one of these at the match when we were fighting the fucking CBeebies, it's fucking loads better than Stonker's Stanley. That'd teach them fucking Chelterton bastards for trolling our fucking Facebook page, all right. I'd be a fucking legend."

Kylie could hear the man's words, but little of what he said made any sense. She knew what CBeebies and Facebook were, but she had never seen either of them. She was too old for watching CBeebies, and Facebook needed either a computer or a phone, neither of which she had ever owned and probably never would. And what did they have to do with what was happening anyway? She thought about the zombie movies she'd seen recently. One of them had Paddy, the vet from Emmerdale, in it. The zombies in that had been similar to the crazies attacking Meadowside, except they barked like dogs and moved a lot faster. Could that really be what they were? Zombies?

"Wait," Kylie said, suddenly thinking of Britney, "why did you ask if I'd been bitten?"

"If you get bit by a zombie, you turn into a zombie. Every fucker knows that."

"But my friend didn't. She just went yellow, then passed out for an hour or so. When she came round she was okay again."

Smiffy shrugged. "Yeah well, it probably takes a while for them to change. But she will, sooner or later, then she'll start chewing down on whoever's nearest to her at the time. Then they'll turn into zombies too. That's how it works. Don't you know nothing?"

Kylie thought about all those people locked up with Britney in the play area. About the other people in there with similar injuries. She hoped what Smiffy was telling her wasn't true, otherwise they would all be dead by now.

"Well," Smiffy said, turning away, "much as I'd like to stand here chatting all day, there's something I need to do. You'd best get yourself somewhere safe before the zombies get you. And if your mate's been bit, stay the fuck away from her."

"What?" Kylie said. "No, wait. You can't leave me here by myself."

Smiffy shrugged as he walked away. "Like I said, I've got something I need to do. You can tag along if you like, I'm not fussed either way. Just don't get under my feet, and keep quiet so you don't attract too many fucking zombies."

Kylie watched Smiffy walk toward the stairs. She looked around for her golf club and picked it up before hurrying after him, stepping gingerly over the mutilated corpses at her feet. Smiffy paused at the bend in the stairway and peered around the corner before continuing down, the chainsaw giving out a steady put-put-put by his side. A lone crazy hissed at him when he emerged from the stairway, blood dripping from its chin down its Argyle jumper. Smiffy smiled and gestured the crazy forward with his fingers.

"Come on then, you fucking cunt. Let's fucking have it."

Smiffy waited until the crazy was almost upon him before he raised the chainsaw. He pulled the trigger and thrust the blades up between the crazy's grasping hands, burying the end in its chest. Smiffy laughed as the crazy flailed its arms, still reaching desperately to grab hold of him. He pulled out the chainsaw and lopped off both the crazy's hands, one after the other, then crouched down and swung the chainsaw at its right leg, just below the knee. The chainsaw screeched as it hit bone, then cut through.

"Timber!" Smiffy shouted as the crazy toppled sideways and fell.

He walked up to the crazy and kicked it in the head when it tried to roll over, sending it spinning onto its back. The crazy thrashed its arms, blood flying in all directions from the ragged stumps where its hands used to be. Smiffy turned to Kylie and nodded.

"You see? You have to get them in the head to kill them. Anywhere else won't fucking work."

Kylie watched the crazy struggle as Smiffy raised his boot above the gaping wound in its chest. "Watch this," Smiffy said, then stamped down. His boot disappeared into the crazy's chest with a crunch followed by a wet squelch, like someone stepping on a giant snail. The crazy's arms shot up like they were spring-loaded, then just as quickly fell to its side. It gave out a rasping sigh, then lay still. Smiffy looked down as he pulled his foot out of the crazy's chest and shook the gore from his boot.

"Well that's interesting," Smiffy said, frowning. "Maybe the movies got that bit wrong? Oh well, it'll make things a lot easier, yeah?" He grinned. "Come on then, kid. Let's get this fucking party started." He looked around at nearby shops, as if he were getting his bearings, then pointed west. "This way, I think."

Smiffy led Kylie through the dimly lit shopping centre in the direction of the war memorial statue. They met sporadic crazies along the way, and Smiffy dispatched them with ruthless efficiency. Most he killed outright with a single slash of the chainsaw to the neck, others he had a little bit more fun with. One man in an expensive-looking suit and tie had his arms and legs hacked off and then left rolling around on the ground to die of blood-loss. Another, a short fat man with a beard, was left with his intestines spilling out of a gaping wound. Smiffy laughed as the man stuffed his own intestines into his mouth, trying to eat them. With others, Smiffy simply sliced off their outstretched fingers and drove the end of the chainsaw sideways into their mouths, then declared them safe enough to come back to later to finish the job.

Kylie watched each death and mutilation numbly, accepting it as necessary but not wanting to get involved. Smiffy seemed mentally unstable, but whether he had always been like that, or if it was a result of the situation they were in, she had no way of knowing. Sometimes he would roar "Skumfuckers!" as he rushed forward to meet a crazy lumbering up to them, other times he would just slash at them with the chainsaw as he passed them by, almost as an afterthought.

When they reached the war memorial statue, Smiffy handed the chainsaw to Kylie. She took it without thinking, surprised at how light it was. Smiffy reached up to the statue and pulled a yellow and red striped scarf from the arm of one of the bronze soldiers. He stretched out the scarf in both hands, then kissed its centre before tying it around his wrist. Kylie noticed there was another identical scarf left hanging from the statue. Smiffy pulled it down and looked around at the mangled corpses littering the ground. Something seemed to catch his eye and he strode up to one of them. Kylie followed, not wanting to be left alone. Smiffy bent down next to an eviscerated body with tatters of yellow clothing sticking to it and looped the scarf through its exposed ribcage.

"Rest in fucking pieces, mate," he said as he tied the scarf in a knot. Then he laughed and walked away.

Kylie followed Smiffy to the nearby exit, carrying Smiffy's chainsaw in one hand and her golf club in the other. Crazies outside pounded on the door and snarled as they approached. Smiffy paused at each corpse he came to and bent down to peer at their remains before moving on. He stopped at one whose arms and legs had been chewed down to the bone, its chest torn open and emptied of its internal organs, its ruined face resembling a lump of raw meat that had been chewed and spat out. Smiffy seemed to recognise the corpse, but Kylie couldn't see how. To her there was nothing to tell one mangled, half-eaten corpse from another.

Smiffy straightened up and looked around. He picked up a blood-soaked scarf he found nearby and wrung it out, then returned to the body and tied it around the bones of its wrist. He picked up the other wrist and dragged the body across the ground to where the other corpse he had recognised lay. He placed them side by side and arranged what was left of them in a more dignified pose, then stood over them and closed his eyes and clasped his hands together in prayer.

"Skumfuckers are in your town," he said quietly, "we'll smash your kneecaps and knock you down. Stick the boot in, stamp on your head. Mess with us and you'll end up dead. So come and have a go with the Skumfucker aggro. Amen." He crossed himself, like a catholic priest, and turned to Kylie. "They were my brothers," he said by way of explanation. "I couldn't leave them without their colours like that, it wouldn't be right."

Kylie heard a wailing, feral cry and spun to face it. A woman staggered toward her, blood dripping from her mouth. Kylie held out the chainsaw for Smiffy.

"No fucking respect for a solemn occasion, these zombie bastards," Smiffy said, stepping around Kylie and ignoring the proffered chainsaw. "Come on then, you rancid bitch, let's fucking have it."

The woman lunged with a hiss and grabbed Smiffy's blood-stained shirt. Smiffy lashed out with the palm of his right hand and drove it into the woman's nose with a crunch. At the same time he hooked his left foot around the woman's right leg and jerked it forward. She toppled backwards, pivoted around Smiffy's knee, and he helped her on her way with a shove to the chest. She sat up and hissed. Smiffy kicked her in the face and put her back down. She rolled over and started to push herself up. Blood and teeth dripped from her mouth as she bared her lips and snarled. Smiffy kicked her arms out from under her and her face hit the wooden flooring with a dull thud. Smiffy raised his boot and stamped down on the back of her head, then kicked and stamped it repeatedly until her skull cracked open and bits of her brain squelched out.

Smiffy looked down at her, nodding to himself, then turned away. He took the chainsaw from Kylie and, without another word, strode off back the way they had come.

14

Sally Jones did her best to soothe her baby daughter Jasmine, but she just wouldn't stop crying. Babies could pick up on the mood of those around them, Sally had read in a parenting magazine she flicked through in the maternity ward a few weeks ago. They knew when you were angry, they knew when you were anxious, and they responded accordingly. So it was no wonder Jasmine was picking up on the fear and hysteria of everyone around her.

For Sally it was the heat that bothered her more than anything. And the smell. All those people cramped inside The House of Fun, shoulder to shoulder, no space to move, sweat pouring from every gland. During the hours they had all been locked in there some of the older people had soiled themselves, adding to the pungent aroma. And the longer they remained in their self-imposed captivity, the more likely Sally would lose control of her own bladder. She had hoped Jasmine's birth would put an end to her need to relieve herself so often, but that didn't seem to be the case.

The police woman, Sally couldn't remember her name, urged everyone to remain calm, told them everything was going to be okay, that help was on its way and would be there shortly. But everyone had seen what those people out there were capable of. Seen with their own eyes the way they killed with their teeth and hands; what they did to their victims' bodies while they were still in their death throes. Sally shuddered at the thought. It was only by chance she had been on the upper floor when it all started. Five minutes earlier and she would have been down there in all the chaos. All the killing.

Zombies, some people called them. Others argued they were mental patients who had escaped from an asylum. One man even said it was God's wrath, that he was punishing all the sinners for allowing homosexual depravity to take place with wanton abandon. Sally didn't see the point of speculating like that. It didn't matter who or what they were, or why they were doing it. All that mattered was keeping her baby safe from them.

Sally was one of the last ones to enter The House of Fun, just before the door was closed and bolted. She had to listen to the pitiful cries of those left outside. The frantic pleading to be let in, the wailing sobs when they were ignored. Then the angry shouts and thumps on the door for what seemed like forever. The police woman had told them to find shelter elsewhere, that there was no more room for them. Sally knew she was right, but that didn't make it any easier listening to those poor people outside.

The police woman had pushed her way through the crowd to the back of the play area, and stood on one of the few remaining items of furniture not piled up against the walls as she tried to calm everyone down. Sally couldn't help thinking how many extra people could have been saved if that furniture had been moved out onto the balcony instead. But it was too late now, the unlucky ones had given up all hope of being allowed in long ago, and had either found somewhere else to hide or fallen victim to the killers.

"Shut that fucking brat up, it's doing my head in!" someone shouted.

Sally turned to look, ready to give the man a piece of her mind, but she couldn't see over the people around her well enough to locate him. Others were yelling at him to show some manners, that they were all suffering and there was no need to be so rude. The man swore at them.

"Apart from anything else," he shouted, "it'll attract them fucking zombies. If she can't keep it quiet we should throw her out before it's too late. She shouldn't have been let in here in the first place."

"Shut up, you heartless old bastard," a woman shouted.

Others voiced their own thoughts of the man, everyone

shouting at once. Some agreed with him, though most disagreed. Sally felt a warm glow at their support for her and baby Jasmine. That there were still decent people in the world, even in a situation like this. There were calls for the man himself to be expelled from the play area, along with anyone else who thought the same way, and sporadic fighting broke out as they argued, causing the tightly packed crowd to undulate as those nearby tried to avoid being hit by a stray fist.

"Stop it!" the police woman shouted, clapping her hands for attention like a teacher in front of an unruly class. "We need to stay calm and civilised. I know it's not ideal, all of us cooped up in here together like this, but we can't allow ourselves to—"

Her voice trailed off, drowned out by screams of panic when someone started banging on the entrance door. Sally startled. She raised a hand to her mouth and gasped, clutched the baby to her chest and tried to back away from the door. But there were too many people pressed up around her to get far. The police woman was shouting something, but the words didn't register. The pounding became more intense, drowning out all other sound. The door shuddered in its frame, the bolts holding it in place rattling with every thud.

Then the door started to splinter. It was just a small crack at first, near the bottom hinge. Then the hinge broke away and the bottom of the door buckled inwards. Grasping hands reached through the gap, groping at the feet of those standing there. Sally pressed herself as far back into the crowd as she could to get out of their reach.

Two men tried to push the door back into place, stamping on the hands reaching under it. But they were no match for the pressure from outside, and the gap beneath the door became wider and wider, the top hinge straining against the increased pressure. They called out for help, and more people surged past Sally to join them. Sally stood immobile, unable to tear her eyes away from the door as the top hinge started to buckle and twist. She knew it wouldn't be long until the hinge gave way, then there would be nothing to stop the killers from surging inside.

15

Snarls and moans came from somewhere inside Mothercare. Kylie hurried past, wanting to get as far away from them as possible, the golf club with the knife attached to it held grimly before her like a scythe. She stopped when she realised Smiffy wasn't following her anymore, and turned back to the shop. Smiffy stood near the doorway, peering into Mothercare through the broken shop-front window.

"Leave it," Kylie said, "we need to get back upstairs."

Smiffy grunted and gestured Kylie away with his free hand, the scarf tied around his wrist waving like a flag. He raised the chainsaw and crunched over glass to step into the shop. Kylie watched nervously, expecting hordes of crazies to swarm over Smiffy at any second. She swore to herself, unsure whether to leave him behind or not, then turned and took a few steps away. Tortured screams echoed from somewhere in the distance. Kylie swore again and turned back to Mothercare.

"For fuck's sake, let's get out of here," she shouted.

"Skumfuckers!" Smiffy yelled from inside Mothercare.

The chainsaw revved, and Kylie listened to it slicing through flesh, grinding through bone. She stepped closer to the shop front, ready to run if her worst fears were founded. A thick trail of congealed blood led inside Mothercare, as if something had been dragged across the carpeted flooring and out of the shop. Clothes racks and shelves had been toppled, their contents scattered. Kylie peered around the doorway.

Smiffy thrust the chainsaw into a young girl's face, silencing her in mid-snarl. The girl hung from the end of the chainsaw like a rag doll as Smiffy lifted her off her feet and flung her at a group of crazies crowded around a closed door to one side of the shop. The girl's head disintegrated when she missed the crazies and hit the wall beside them. The crazies took no notice and continued banging on the door as if nothing had happened.

Smiffy ran toward them. He was almost upon them when one turned with a startled roar and lunged forward, hands outstretched. Smiffy held the chainsaw out before him and laughed as the crazy impaled itself on it. The crazy's teeth gnashed at Smiffy's face as it pushed itself closer to him along the length of the spinning blades. The chainsaw erupted from the crazy's back in a shower of blood and flying lumps of flesh. Smiffy wrenched the chainsaw up into the crazy's chest, slicing through vital organs, and kicked out with his foot as he pulled the chainsaw back out of its body. The crazy fell. Smiffy went for the remaining ones in front of the door.

He crouched low and swung the chainsaw at waist height at the one closest to him. The chainsaw ripped through the crazy's torso, spilling its intestines as it fell. In one fluid movement Smiffy jerked back the chainsaw and thrust it between the legs of another crazy. He straightened up as he wrenched the chainsaw up through the man's groin, screeching through his pelvis and up into his stomach.

A female crazy grabbed Smiffy from behind and moved in to bite. Kylie called out a warning, but it wasn't needed. Smiffy spun around, holding the chainsaw in both hands. The chainsaw ripped out of the first crazy's stomach and tore into the woman's side. Smiffy roared as he used the momentum to slice her in half.

The remaining crazy bared its teeth and hissed. It raised its hands and formed claws with its fingers, then lurched at Smiffy. Smiffy tilted the chainsaw sideways and rammed it into the crazy's mouth, then pushed it down its throat. The crazy stumbled back, its arms flailing, as blood and teeth flew from the chainsaw's spinning blades. Smiffy jerked the chainsaw to one side and it erupted from the crazy's cheek. He whooped and spun a full circle with the chainsaw held out before him, then slashed through the crazy's neck. The crazy's head toppled to one side, held on by a few tendons as blood geysered out of its neck. Smiffy laughed as the crazy fell to its knees and toppled forward. He swung his leg back and kicked it in the head. Tendons snapped and the head rolled across the carpet. When it came to a halt its lifeless eyes stared at Kylie accusingly.

"That's the fucking way to do it," Smiffy said. He turned to leave, and smiled at Kylie standing by the broken shop-front window as he walked toward her. "Fucking smart or what?" he said. "Stick with me kid, we'll soon get rid of all these fucking zombie bastards."

An odd sound, like a cat mewling, came from behind the closed door. Smiffy turned back to it and cocked his head to one side like a confused dog. "What the fuck's that?" he asked, and walked up to the door and put his ear against it.

Kylie walked into the shop, curious herself at what might be causing such a sound. Smiffy twisted the door handle and pushed, but the door was locked. He stepped back and kicked it. The door rattled in its frame, but held strong. He kicked it a couple more times, then gave up and used the chainsaw to cut around the lock before kicking it again. The door flew open and slammed back on its hinges. Smiffy stepped inside and revved the chainsaw.

Kylie was about to join Smiffy when she tasted the strong stench of piss, shit and blood coming from the room. She gagged and held her hand over her nose and mouth as she turned away.

"Get in here, kid," Smiffy shouted. "I reckon I might need some help with this."

"What is it?" Kylie asked.

Smiffy switched off the chainsaw. "Come and see for yourself."

Kylie forced down her revulsion and stepped into the room, still covering her mouth and nose. It was a store room, about ten feet by twenty feet, and toppled cardboard boxes littered the floor. She stepped around them gingerly and headed to where Smiffy stood crouched over something in one corner of the room. As she got closer she saw it was just another dead body, and wondered what was so special about it. She had lost count of the number of mutilated corpses she had seen that day, and now looked at them with a casual detachment.

"What am I supposed to be looking at?" Kylie asked.

Then she heard the odd mewling sound again. It came from the corpse behind Smiffy. Kylie climbed over the remaining boxes blocking her way and looked down. A naked woman stared up lifelessly, a thick pool of blood spreading from between her legs. In the crook of one arm, wrapped in what Kylie assumed was the woman's clothing, lay a blood-encrusted baby. Its deep blue eyes seemed impossibly large for its tiny head as it looked up at Kylie and whimpered, its bottom lip quivering.

Kylie leaned her golf club against a nearby box, then bent down and picked the baby up. She felt resistance as she tried to cradle it to her chest, and opened up the bundle of clothing it was wrapped in. The umbilical cord was still attached, the other end disappearing into the woman's huge, torn vagina. Kylie looked at Smiffy. Smiffy nodded.

"That's what I were needing help with. Any idea what to do?"

Kylie thought back to a childbirth video she had been forced to watch in biology at school. It was the most disgusting thing she had ever seen, far worse than any horror movie. One girl had even fainted, another swore she would never have sex with anyone ever again for as long as she lived. Kylie suspected that was the reason they were shown the video, in an attempt to cut down on the number of pregnancies at the school. But what had they done after the baby was born? She remembered them wrapping it in a big towel, but what happened to the umbilical cord? Kylie couldn't remember if they showed that part or not before the camera cut away to the afterbirth scene. That was even more gross, like a huge slab of raw meat being squeezed out of the woman's privates.

"Well?" Smiffy asked. "What do we do?"

Kylie looked between the woman's legs, but she couldn't see any signs of afterbirth.

"I don't know," she said, shaking her head. "I think there's another bit still inside her that needs to come out first?"

Smiffy grunted and bent down to the woman. He picked up the umbilical cord trailing out of her vagina and tugged on it. His hands slipped along its length, unable to gain any grip. He wrapped the cord around his fingers and tried again, but with no success. The cord stretched, but stubbornly refused to come out of the woman's vagina. Smiffy dropped the umbilical cord and sighed, then took the baby from Kylie and pulled on that instead. The baby screamed, thrashing its tiny arms and legs.

"Stop, you're hurting it," Kylie shouted.

"For fuck's sake," Smiffy said, handing the baby back to Kylie. "We have to get it off her somehow."

Kylie cradled the baby and rocked it as it continued screaming. Smiffy picked up the chainsaw and thumbed its ignition switch.

"Stretch it out again," he shouted as he revved it. "It's no good, I'm going to have to cut the fucker off."

Kylie stepped back, holding the baby upright before her in both hands, hoping this was the right thing to do. When the umbilical cord was stretched out tight, Smiffy gripped it in one hand, about six inches away from the baby. He glanced at Kylie, nodded, then raised the chainsaw to the umbilical cord. It ripped through with ease and twanged back toward the woman's vagina like a striking snake. Kylie stumbled a few steps before she regained her balance, then looked down at the baby. She had expected the umbilical cord to be gushing blood like a hosepipe, but only a few small drops formed where it had been severed. She squeezed the end of the cord between her thumb and forefinger to stop the bleeding. It felt soft and squishy, slightly warm, and not at all how she imagined it would.

Smiffy glanced at the baby, then kicked boxes out of his way and went back into the shop.

"Well come on then, kid," he said, "let's get fucked off. Them zombie bastards won't kill themselves, will they?"

Kylie looked around the store room for a clean blanket to wrap the baby in, then followed him out.

16

Kylie didn't know what she was supposed to do with the baby. Smiffy didn't seem to care, he was more interested in killing crazies than anything else and did so with relish as soon as they got close enough. The baby cried constantly, and ignored all Kylie's attempts to soothe it. This attracted more and more crazies for Smiffy to hack to pieces, so it seemed odd to Kylie that he would keep yelling at the baby to shut the fuck up.

"I think it might be hungry," Kylie said.

"Well feed it then," Smiffy yelled above the roar of the chainsaw as he slashed through another crazy.

"What with?"

"How the fuck should I know? Milk or something."

"I think we should take it to that police woman, she'll know what to do."

Smiffy finished off the crazy and turned to look at Kylie. His brow furrowed. "What police woman?"

"Didn't you hear the message, saying everyone should make their way upstairs?"

Smiffy shrugged. "Nah, must have been busy killing zombies at the time. So where is she then?"

"She's got everyone locked inside The House of Fun until the rest of the police arrive."

Smiffy laughed. "Yeah, that sounds about right. Coppers are a bunch of fucking cowards when they're on their own, but when they're mob-handed they'll crack your head open just for looking at them funny. Listen kid, I wouldn't waste your time on some fucking copper, they're all thick as pig shit." Smiffy laughed again. "Pig shit, get it?"

Kylie frowned. "My friends are there too. Mike and Britney. They're all I've got now that—" her voice trailed off into a sob as she thought about Tom.

Smiffy sighed, then nodded. He clapped a hand on

Kylie's shoulder. "Yeah, okay, fair enough. Friends are important, and you should be with them. So where's this House of Fun place then?"

Kylie led the way through the shopping centre, back the way they had come. As they approached the escalator she had helped board up with Tom and the four men they had met she gasped. The escalator's glass sides were awash with blood, the steps littered with the bodies of fallen crazies. But the makeshift barrier at the top had been torn down, giving the remaining crazies easy access to the upper floor. Of those there was no sign, but shouts and screams coming from the direction of The House of Fun told Kylie everything she needed to know.

"We need to get up there quick," she yelled.

Smiffy nodded grimly. He walked up to the escalator and stepped over the statue lying at its base. He almost lost his footing as he slipped on something, and grabbed the handrail to steady himself. Corpses lay in his way, and he had no choice but to climb over them to reach the next clear step. He hooked the chainsaw over the side of the escalator and clung on to the opposite handrail as he stepped onto the first body. The body rolled under his weight and he swore as he tried to regain his balance, his feet slipping from beneath him. Once he was on firm ground again he tossed the chainsaw a few steps further up and held onto the handrails with both hands until he reached it. Then he tossed it a bit further and continued his assent to the top, where he turned and waited for Kylie.

Kylie climbed gingerly over the first corpse. She clung to the handrail with her leading hand and inched her way sideways up the escalator with the baby held firmly to her chest. She knew she couldn't afford to stumble, that she would crush the baby if she did, just like the woman who had attacked Britney had crushed hers when Tom pushed her over. Smiffy held out his hand for her as she neared the top, and helped her climb over the last of the bodies. Once she was clear, Kylie snatched her hand away and hurried to The House of Fun, dreading what she would find there.

Kylie's worst fears were realised when she saw a huge mob of hissing and snarling crazies surrounding the play area entrance. They spilled out to cover the entire walkway in both directions, and fought amongst themselves to reach the small doorway in the middle. The door itself seemed to be loose, and buckled wildly as crazies pushed against it.

At the opposite side to where Kylie and Smiffy approached The House of Fun, a large group of men and women attacked the outer fringe of the crazies with makeshift weapons. They clubbed them with baseball bats, stabbed them with carving knives, hacked at them with axes and shovels, shattered their skulls with hammers. One heavily-built man wearing a motorcycle crash helmet and full body leathers even fought bare-handed. He wrestled a crazy to the ground, smashed out its teeth using the metal-plated knuckle protectors on his leather gloves, then lifted it above his head and hurled it over the balcony. The crazy hissed as it fell, its hands grasping upwards, then landed with a crack as its head split open on the wooden flooring below.

"Skumfuckers!" Smiffy yelled, and ran at the crazies with his chainsaw roaring.

Crazies turned in his direction, then hissed as one. Smiffy thrust the chainsaw into the face of one, and kicked out at another. His boot struck the crazy on the knee and snapped its leg. As the crazy lurched to one side Smiffy wrenched the chainsaw out of the first crazy's ruined face and swung it down into the second crazy's neck. It sliced through with ease and the crazy fell, showering those nearby with arterial blood, its head lolling to one side. Some of the crazies ignored the commotion, too eager to reach the doorway before them. Others turned and hissed, then stumbled toward Smiffy with their arms outstretched.

Smiffy swung the chainsaw before him, back and forth in a wide arc, slicing through crazies as they approached him. Grasping hands were severed. Stomachs were torn open, spilling foul-smelling intestines at his feet. Child-size crazies were decapitated. Blood and gore flew from the chainsaw's spinning blades like strawberry jelly. Smiffy laughed as bodies toppled and fell all around him, forming a barrier between him and the remaining crazies around the doorway. He kicked and stamped on the ones still moving, climbed over the ones that lay still. All the while his chainsaw slashed at the ones still standing between him and the door.

The other fighters were also making good progress with their makeshift weapons, but their advancement through the crowd of crazies was nowhere near as fast as Smiffy's. Those with blunt weapons bludgeoned the crazies unconscious, then followed the motorcyclist's lead and tossed them over the balcony. The ones with sharper implements hacked and slashed, leaving bodies where they fell.

The door to The House of Fun gave way and dozens of crazies surged inside. Frantic cries of fear turned into screams of agony as people were torn apart and devoured.

Smiffy and the other fighters, all drenched in blood and gore, made for the doorway together, slashing at crazies as they went. Kylie was worried that Smiffy, in his blind killing frenzy, would attack the other fighters, but he seemed to sense they were on his side and lowered his chainsaw just as they came within reach of its spinning blades.

Smiffy rushed through the door first, shouting his Skumfuckers battle cry, closely followed by other fighters. Kylie heard the chainsaw slicing through flesh, grating against bone, the sound of axes hacking through flesh. Some of the fighters remained outside and finished off any crazies who were still rolling around trying to get back up despite their injuries. One startled when he saw Kylie standing nearby, and raised a blood-stained baseball bat defensively. His eyes widened at the baby cradled in her arms. His mouth hung open. An injured crazy hissed up at him. He turned away from Kylie and slammed the baseball bat down into its face.

Smiffy's chainsaw slowed to an idle, then stopped altogether. Shouts came from inside the play area. A woman told everyone to lower their weapons. Kylie weaved around the dead crazies littering the balcony and splashed through their blood to make her way to the entrance, desperate to be reunited with Mike and Britney.

Smiffy walked out of the play area, grinning. The hand with the scarf tied around it was clenched in a fist and raised before him in a sign of victory, the silent chainsaw held by his side. He winked at Kylie as he splashed past her, then leaned against the balcony and faced the doorway while ashen-faced survivors walked out.

The first was the police woman, who ordered everyone to put their weapons down. She was followed by an elderly man and woman in their mid-sixties, and a young girl not much older than seven or eight, accompanied by a woman Kylie assumed was the girl's mother. More walked out, some with minor injuries.

Kylie stood staring at the doorway, willing Mike and Britney to walk through it. She shouted their names when they didn't appear, and when nobody else came out she ran to the opening.

Inside, the entrance to the play area was awash with the bloodied remains of dismembered crazies and their fallen, partially-consumed victims. More bodies lay beyond them, among splinters of broken furniture they had tried to hide behind. The remaining fighters crouched over them, searching for survivors, their weapons abandoned.

"Mike! Britney! Where are you?" Kylie yelled.

One of the fighters, his face drenched in blood, looked up and locked eyes with Kylie. The body he crouched before gave out a gurgling groan.

"Kylie?" he said with a shaking voice.

"Tom!" Kylie yelled, and rushed into the play area.

"No, wait there," Tom said quickly.

Kylie hesitated, then stepped gingerly between the corpses, looking down so she wouldn't lose her footing in the slippery mess. Once she was past them she looked up at Tom. He had his hands around someone's neck, blood spurting between his fingers.

"Tom, who–" Kylie's voice trailed off when she saw patches of pink between the splashes of blood covering the girl's clothing. "Britney? BRITNEY!" She rushed forward and knelt by her side. "Oh god, Britney!"

Britney's eyes flickered open. Her breath came in a rasping gurgle. Most of her nose was missing, the rest of her face a mass of raw, torn flesh. Blood bubbled from between Tom's fingers when she exhaled.

"What do we do?" Kylie asked, frantic.

Tom shook his head slowly. Tears rolled down his face. "I'm sorry Kylie, it's too late for that."

"No, it can't be," Kylie said, rising to her feet. I'll go and get that police woman, she'll know what to do."

"You need to say goodbye. It's too late for anything else, she hasn't got long left."

Kylie looked down at Britney as she gave out a final, rasping breath. Her eyes stared up, unseeing. Kylie dropped to her knees, the baby cradled in one arm. Tom wiped his bloody hands on his tracksuit bottoms and reached out to embrace her. Kylie sobbed into his chest, not caring about the sticky blood smeared all over him.

She broke away when the baby pressed between them started crying again. "Where's Mike?" she asked. But the look on Tom's face told her everything she needed to know. She melted back into his arms and he held her tight.

Outside, the police woman shouted for everyone's attention. Kylie raised her head and looked at Tom.

"We'd best go and see what she wants," he said softly, and pulled Kylie to her feet. He opened a fold of the baby's blanket and peered at its face. The baby gurgled up at him, oblivious to the horror around it. Tom wiped his nose and attempted a smile, but it seemed forced. "Come on then, Kylie."

As they left The House of Fun Kylie saw the police woman surrounded by dozens of people, their weapons discarded as they listened to what she had to say. Only Smiffy seemed uninterested, and leaned over the balcony looking down, the chainsaw propped up by his feet.

"The police or the army will be here to sort things out soon," the police woman said, "so until they get here this is what we're going to do. It might take them a few days to reach us, so we may need to take emergency supplies from some of the shops while we wait. We'll keep a record of anything we take so the shop owners can be reimbursed at a later date. I'll also need a list of everyone's names and addresses, so that–"

"Fuck that," Smiffy said, turning toward her and shaking his head. He pushed himself away from the balcony and stepped forward. "Who the fuck put you in charge, lady? The way I see it, we just saved your fucking life so that means we tell *you* what to do, not the other way round." He pushed his way through the crowd, nudging people out of the way until he stood before the police woman.

"I'm a police officer. In a state of emergency like this I have the power to–"

Smiffy lunged forward and grabbed her by the neck with one hand. "Lady, I don't give a fuck what you are," he said with a sneer, "I'm in charge here, not you. I'm the fucking zombie slayer, and what I say goes."

The police woman's eyes bulged. Her tongue lolled from her mouth as she gasped for air. She grasped at Smiffy's hand and kicked out at his ankles, squirming to free herself from his grip. Smiffy punched her in the face with his free hand, then punched her again. Her eyes rolled up in their sockets and her arms fell limp by her sides.

Someone tried to pull Smiffy off her, shouting for him to let her go. Smiffy backhanded the man and sent him spinning away. He dragged the police woman by the neck up to the balcony and pushed her back against it, then punched her in the face again a few more times. Still holding her by the neck with one hand, he bent down and crooked his other arm under her knees, then lifted her onto the balcony's edge and hurled her over. She fell silently, tumbling through the air, and landed in a tangled heap of splayed arms and legs.

Smiffy nodded to himself, then spat over the balcony at the crumpled body below. He turned to face the shocked crowd, who were edging away from him. He rubbed his hands together and smiled.

"Fucking bastard coppers thinking they can still push us around. Right then, this is what we're *really* going to do."

A man picked up an axe and raised it above his head, then ran at Smiffy with a roar. Smiffy spun to face him, his fists raised. His eyes widened as the axe hurtled toward him. He raised his hands to protect his face and the axe thudded into his chest, shattering through his ribcage. Smiffy fell to his knees, staring down at the axe embedded in his chest, the blood pouring down its wooden handle. He looked up at the man who had put it there with a confused look, then toppled forward.

Kylie turned away and reached out for Tom. He held her tight and she hoped he would never let go.

Epilogue

Kylie sat on a luxury leather sofa near the war memorial statue, watching Tom and Britney playing together in the dim emergency lighting. Expensive toys of all kinds were scattered everywhere, but Britney favoured the small die-cast cars and green plastic soldiers she had found in a bargain bin a year ago. She stood the soldiers in a line, then ran them over with the cars. When they were all knocked over she would stand them up again and start over. This was the only game Britney had played since finding the soldiers, her other toys lying forgotten all around her. Kylie had asked her once why she had stopped playing with her other toys.

"Bad men outside," was Britney's response. "Need to kill them."

That had been the first time Britney had ever mentioned the crazies. Kylie and Tom had done their best to shield them from her by never going anywhere near the exit doors, where they still pounded relentlessly, day and night. Kylie wondered what else Britney had picked up on during her short life in Meadowside.

Britney was almost two years old, and full of curiosity about everything. Several times now, Kylie and Tom had woken to find her missing from her cot. They had no idea how she got over the bars, and the first time it happened they thought she had been taken by a crazy they had somehow missed. After a frantic search they found her by the war memorial statue. Something seemed to draw her to the bronze soldiers, because that was where she would end up every time she went missing. So eventually Kylie and Tom moved their home into one of the nearby shops, and the area around the statue became Britney's permanent playground.

After the last of the crazies inside Meadowside had been killed, there was the problem of what to do with them. They couldn't just leave them to rot, the smell would have been too overpowering, and the risk of disease too great. At first someone had suggested burning them in the open space around the food hall, but that idea was soon dismissed due to fears of the fire spreading. Someone else suggested throwing them off the roof, which sounded like a good idea, but nobody knew how to get up there. In the end they had smashed the outside windows of upper floor shops and tossed them out to the hungry crazies below, then boarded the windows up.

After that, everyone had gone their separate ways and found their own little corner of Meadowside to live in. Tom and Kylie hardly ever saw any of the other survivors, except the odd one or two while they were out shopping for supplies. They nodded in recognition, but nobody ever engaged in conversation anymore. They knew the only topic would be what they had all gone through, and nobody wanted to be reminded of those days.

"Need a piss," Britney announced, standing up.

Kylie was about to rise from the sofa when Tom said he would take her. She settled back down again and smiled as she watched him lead Britney away. Tom had been a great father to the child, and it made Kylie love him all the more for it. He was nothing like Kylie's own father, who had just been a pissed up waster all her life. She knew Tom would be over the moon when she told him she was pregnant. She had done the test earlier that morning, and was just waiting for the right moment to tell him the good news.

Rapid gunfire came from somewhere in the distance. Kylie jumped up and looked around, trying to locate where it had come from.

"Tom?" she yelled.

When he didn't reply, Kylie ran to the nearby public

toilets and burst through the door. Tom leaned against a sink, watching Britney perched on the edge of a toilet in one of the cubicles, swinging her legs backwards and forwards.

"Did you hear that?" Kylie asked.

"Hear what?" Tom said with a shrug.

Britney climbed off the toilet and bent down in front of Tom. "Arse wipe," she demanded. Tom picked up one of the stash of toilet rolls they kept in there and wrapped a wad of paper round his hand. He wiped Britney clean, then tossed it into the toilet and flushed it away.

The rapid gunfire came again, closely followed by a loud explosion.

"What the fuck was that?" Tom asked, turning to look at Kylie.

"Bang bang," Britney said. "Kill bad men."

"I don't know," Kylie said, shaking her head, "but we'd better go and see."

Other survivors had heard it too, and had congregated near the north exit when Kylie, Tom and Britney got there. Some of them brandished tools as weapons, and looked at each other nervously. The crazies had moved away from the doors, giving everyone a clear view of the car park beyond. The tarmac was pock-marked with explosions, littered with the charred remains of dead crazies. Some of the living crazies were feeding on them, but most were shuffling away into the distance, where sporadic gunshots still rang out.

"It's got to be the army," a man said, excitedly. "Who else would have guns and bombs out there?"

There were murmurs of agreement. "They've come to save us!" a woman shouted.

"I wouldn't be so sure about that if I were you," Dan Foster said, leaning on his walking stick. Everyone turned to look at him as he raised the walking stick and pointed at the exit door. "It could be any fucker out there for all we know. All I'm saying is, we shouldn't be in too much of a hurry to welcome them, whoever they are. We should stay out of sight until we know who they are and what they want."

"Oh come on," the woman argued, "you can't be serious? After all this time there's been nobody, and now when we're rescued you want to hide away from them?"

Dan shrugged. "Well it's up to you. If you want to take the risk, you go ahead. Me, I'm going to wait and see. Besides, even if they *are* army, if you go running up to them they'll just assume you're a zombie and shoot you."

"He's right," Tom said. "They'll shoot first and ask questions later, that's what I'd do in their position."

While they were arguing, a vehicle approached at high speed, its tyres squealing around the bend leading into the car park. Kylie picked up Britney and ran into a nearby shop with Tom. The others looked at each other in silence, then peeled away to find hiding places of their own when another gunshot rang out. The last of them was just out of sight when the glass doors shattered. Kyle put Britney down and crept to the front of the shop to watch through the shutters.

A small boy crunched over broken glass into Meadowside, followed by a young woman in army fatigues. She looked around, pointing the rifle in all directions, then picked up the boy and ran to a nearby escalator.

"It's the army," Kylie said. "They've come to rescue us."

Tom joined her at the front of the shop. They watched through the shutters together as another man stepped through the door into Meadowside. At first Kylie thought he was one of the crazies, due to his wild, staring eyes and his dishevelled appearance. But he was overweight, whereas all the crazies outside were emaciated, and he carried a baseball bat and an axe with him.

"What do we do?" Kylie whispered.

"I don't know," Tom said, "let's wait and see what

happens."

But others were already emerging from their hiding places. The dishevelled man stood still and watched, his eyes flitting nervously between them. He raised his axe and stepped closer.

"No, it's okay," a woman said, palms held out to the man. "You're safe here."

The man stopped again, then licked his cracked, dry lips. "Are you, um... I mean, are..." His face turned red and he looked down at his feet. "Are you... um... well?"

"Yes, we all are. But we need to seal off that door before the zombies get in. Is there anyone else with you?"

"Um... no, just me."

The woman, and two of the men with her, went into one of the nearby shops and came out with arms full of metal display shelving. They skirted around the dishevelled man and headed for the exit door, then piled the shelves up around it.

Tom and Kylie stepped out of the shop. Tom went to help the others barricade the door, while Kylie picked up Britney and headed for the escalator. The woman and child stared down at her, open-mouthed. Kylie smiled up at her.

"I'm Kylie, this is Britney," she said as she walked up the escalator. "Are you in the army? Will the others be here soon?"

The woman shook her head. "No. There's nobody left out there, they're all dead. It's just those things left out there now." The boy started to cry, and the woman picked him up. "I'm Lynn. This is my son, Tommy."

"Hello Tommy," Kylie said, smiling at the boy. "You're going to like living here, there's lots of toys to play with and everything. And I bet you like chocolate, don't you? Well there's lots of that here too."

"Is it safe here?" Lynn asked.

Kylie looked down at the exit door and nodded. "It is now."

Also available by Marcus Blakeston:

Punk Faction
Skinhead Away
Bare Knuckle Bitch
Punk Rock Nursing Home
Biker Sluts versus Flying Saucers
Runaway

Printed in Great Britain
by Amazon